Katie never forgot for a moment that Brian was there beside her, that they were running together. There seemed to be a natural rhythm common to them both. She felt it in the way they instinctively matched pace, their feet coming to the pavement in the same instant, as if to a beat. She felt it in the flow of their arms and shoulders, close, in unison, moving ahead. He seemed a part of her. She could not have assigned a name to what he was—friend, companion, sweetheart. He was not really any of those, or he was all of those, in the short, sweet hours they ran together.

Dear Readers,

We at Silhouette would like to thank all our readers for your many enthusiastic letters. In direct response to your encouragement, we are now publishing *four* FIRST LOVEs every month.

As always FIRST LOVEs are written especially for and about you—your hopes, your dreams, your ambitions.

Please continue to share your suggestions and comments with us; they play an important part in our pleasing you.

I invite you to write to us at the address below:

Nancy Jackson
Senior Editor
Silhouette Books
P.O. Box 769
New York, N.Y. 10019

LOVE ON THE RUN
Leslie Graham

First Love from Silhouette
Published by Silhouette Books New York
America's Publisher of Contemporary Romance

SILHOUETTE BOOKS, a Division of Simon & Schuster, Inc.
1230 Avenue of the Americas, New York, N.Y. 10020

Copyright © 1983 by Leslie Graham

Distributed by Pocket Books

All rights reserved, including the right to reproduce
this book or portions thereof in any form whatsoever.
For information address Silhouette Books, 1230
Avenue of the Americas, New York, N.Y. 10020

ISBN: 0-671-53355-X

First Silhouette Books printing July, 1983

10 9 8 7 6 5 4 3 2 1

All of the characters in this book are fictitious. Any resemblance to actual persons, living or dead, is purely coincidental.

SILHOUETTE, SILHOUETTE ROMANCE and colophon are
registered trademarks of Simon & Schuster, Inc.

America's Publisher of Contemporary Romance

Printed in the U.S.A.

LOVE ON THE RUN

1

It was the first day of school after Easter, and the California sun was shining as if Monday were still a holiday. Katie Marshall couldn't help feeling good as she walked to school with her friend DeeDee. She'd caught her hair back with a blue ribbon that matched her shoes, and she'd dusted her cheeks with the lightest touch of peach blusher—and DeeDee had noticed. In the grass at the edge of the little neighborhood park she saw some late wild flowers—golden poppies and bright clumps of Indian paintbrush. And Katie loved flowers.

Then one of the junior boys had given her and DeeDee a lift in his VW Bug, and the first thing he said was, "Hey, Katie, new shoes. Great!"

He was right. Those running shoes, in two shades of blue with the single white stripe that swooped like a wave across the sides, were absolutely great. They were what she had begged for at Easter—"not a new dress, *please.*" Then, in the very same shoes during ten o'clock gym she broke her own time for six laps around the track. And at eleven o'clock she got an *A* for her paper on Jane Austen from Miss Cummings, just about her favorite teacher next to Coach Miles.

So it should have been a perfect morning. In a way, it was: She'd almost forgotten the events of Easter weekend at home. But now it was lunchtime, and reality was about to descend; would she get through the next hour without anyone knowing that her life had taken a disastrous, hopeless plunge? Well, anyone but DeeDee, of course; but then, DeeDee knew everything about her. As for the rest of the world, she was embarking that very moment on a course designed to keep them from the grim truths of Katie Marshall's life. Her task began in earnest when she opened her lunchbox, took one look at its contents and then fled her circle of friends seated on the grassy slope of the inner court that was the sophomore hangout. Even DeeDee didn't catch her leaving.

Katie headed straight for the covered area just outside the cafeteria. An architect had designed it for pleasant eating—an arbor with redwood tables and benches and climbing wisteria vines for shade. But like lots of designers, he hadn't the faintest idea of how social life really worked in a high school. His award-winning "lounge eating area— Linda Vista High School" had ended up as the place where the freshman class was relegated, at least until they knew their way around, and there they were joined only by misfits of one kind or another. It was known by students and teachers alike as Poker Flats, or simply, the Flats, because in fact that's exactly where the outcasts went, where they were herded and where they huddled, alone and miserable.

Katie went there to hide. She'd had her turn as a frosh there last year and hadn't expected ever to set foot in the Flats again, but today was different. She had a note that excused her from school that afternoon on "needed family business," and she sought the Flats as the best place to hide while she waited for her mother to pick her up. In its shadows, behind the sunny benches, she could stand unobserved, ready to dash out when Mom appeared—with the other occupant of the car.

First, though, there was the matter of her lunch-box. She went over to a big trash can, and there, making sure no one was looking, she opened the box and pulled out two huge chocolate Easter eggs. Gross. They were really gross. They were home-made, that was for sure—all funny and lumpy, not even the same size. They were decorated with sticky green and white flowers with pink handwriting that said, incredibly, "Katie-doll" on one and on the other, "Katie-did."

Gran had made them, of course. When? Katie couldn't imagine. Her grandmother had arrived Saturday afternoon. She'd gone to sleep at seven o'clock that night. "It's been a long trip, my dears," she had said. "Too long for an old woman." Then, the next morning, she had gone to church with all of them. She had taken a nap when they returned, then got up and ate Easter dinner.

In fact, she had made raisin sauce for the ham which Dad said was the best he'd ever tasted and just like the old days, and then, at least so Katie remembered, she had gone straight to bed again.

Well, sometime in the middle of the night she must have gotten up and made big, funny, dumb Easter eggs and made Mom put them in Katie's lunch—like she was in the fifth grade or something, not a sophomore in high school, fifteen years old. Katie took one more look at the eggs and dumped them through the swinging top of the trash can, feeling a twinge as she did so. Not just for DeeDee, who perished at the thought of chocolate in any form and would truly have mourned the loss of these two thick hunks of the pure stuff, but also, Katie knew, for a part of herself: the Katie who once, years ago, when she was—what?—five, maybe, had loved the grandmother who crooned to her over and over, "Katie-doll, my Katie-did."

But she hadn't seen this grandmother for ten years, and if time had stood still for Gran, it hadn't for Katie. She could imagine the shouts of laughter (maybe even from the loyal DeeDee) if the chocolate eggs had ever emerged from her lunchbox. So Katie stood there beside the trash can watching intently every car that came. Here in the shadows it was a little hard to see. But she was determined not to be seen until the last minute, when she would have to run out to the car where an old woman would surely be leaning out the window calling, "Over here, Katie-doll!"

A small blue station wagon drove up, and she almost ran out. It wasn't theirs. She turned back and saw that the kids in Poker Flats were getting

up, milling around. Someone was hollering.
"Come on, frosh—up and out! Rally time in the
amphitheater!"

Katie turned her back quickly against that voice,
for she knew it well. Brian Foster, president of the
senior class, track star, straight *A* student and the
hero of too many of her dreams—that's who was
calling the freshmen to rally. Desperately she
shrank against the wall, hoping he wouldn't see
her—Katie Marshall alone in the Flats.

But he did; of course he did. "Hey there, you
with the blue ribbon. We want all freshmen out on
the double!" His voice came nearer, and suddenly
she felt a hand on her shoulder. "Let's get going,
kid," he said as he swung her around.

And there she was, looking straight at Brian
Foster, face to face, close, for the first time in her
life. She couldn't speak. And for a moment he said
nothing. Then, "Hey, I know you," he said.
"You're not a freshman. You're a soph. I know—
DeeDee. No, no, DeeDee's your friend. You two
just joined the Joggers Club." Then his face broke
into a grin. "I've got it. You're Kate Marshall,
that's who. Katie."

Dumbly she nodded. Her heart was thumping.
Why couldn't she say something—anything?

"Well, for Pete's sake," he said, still grinning,
"what's a girl like you doing in the Flats?"

"Is there some law against being here if I want to
be?" she burst out. It was the first thing she could
think of, the only thing. Helplessly she realized it
was all wrong; she sounded flip and cross and
grumpy all at the same time. No wonder Brian
looked surprised.

"Look," he said, "you've got me wrong. I just thought you'd like to go to the rally."

"Well, I can't. I have to meet someone." She sounded crosser than ever. "I have to wait right here." And like a little girl, too.

"I see," he said. "Sure. Sorry."

He seemed to be staring at her as if he were seeing her for the first time. Maybe he was. But she didn't need to look at him to see every detail of the six-feet-two that was Brian Foster: the light blue eyes, the tan face, the blond hair, barely sun-bleached, that curled close to his neck and just hid the tops of his ears. She even could have described the sweater he wore that morning with his faded denims. It was a rope-stitch cotton crew neck, fisherman's style, and she'd seen him pull it off and toss it to one of the senior girls who had watched the morning workouts from the bleachers. "Take it if you're cold," he'd called, and of course the girl had wrapped it around her shoulders like a precious gift. Katie would have done the same.

Now he was speaking to her in almost the same friendly tone. It was a way he had, she'd noticed, as if he were truly thinking of the other person, as if he cared about them, whoever they were.

"Why don't you wait outside there in the sun," he said. "Hey, look, it's a great day. You don't want to hang around in this place." He took her hand suddenly and started to walk her out toward the drive. Her head felt light, her hand in his like a separate, floating part of her. If the moment could have lasted forever, she would have been content.

But then, disaster. A horn honked. From the corner of her eye Katie saw that this blue station wagon was hers, no way out of that. There was a black dog hanging out the rear window—and that was not all.

"I've got to go," she said desperately, trying to move. But Brian Foster kept a firm grip on her hand.

"Wait a minute, Kate, I'll go with you," he said, and he started to do just that. Then somehow Katie broke away and ran, racing for the car, knowing, her heart sinking, that she would not be in time.

And she was not. For as she reached the door and heard Brian call again, "Wait! Please, Kate . . ." she also heard the very words she'd tried so hard to keep as her own mortifying secret:

"Katie-doll! Gran's Katie-doll." The greeting rang out in the driveway.

Horrified, Katie got into the rear seat and sank against the big dog without a backward glance.

What Katie Marshall was needed at home for on that sunny spring afternoon was to stay with her grandmother. To babysit. It might as well be called by the right word. She had to babysit her grandmother, a grown woman. And she would have to whenever Mom and Dad said so—on and on. She'd probably never get to go anywhere again. That's the way it seemed to her, and that's what she had blurted to her parents—and then felt awful about —the night they'd had a family council so long ago.

Or at least it seemed long ago. Actually fate had dealt Katie its cruel blow only weeks before, and this particular council had taken place only days ago. And the cruel blow, she knew, had not been to her at all but to her grandmother. Grandfather

Marshall had died suddenly, and Dad had gone east to be with his mother. Katie remembered Mom saying, "You must ask her to come right to us, John. She mustn't be alone."

That seemed all right to Katie. She didn't really think very much about it. Then the few weeks it took Gran's sister to help her close the house back east were over, and Katie began to understand the change that was to come over her own house. Gran was coming to live with the Marshalls. They would become what Dad called an extended family. When a father and mother and children lived all by themselves, Mom explained, they were a nuclear family, but extended families included grandparents or other relatives and made homes much nicer places to live in.

What was the matter with that? There was plenty of room: There were four bedrooms in the house on Ivy Lane in Linda Vista. The Marshalls lived in the part of the San Francisco Bay area called simply the Peninsula, and Dad was a project engineer who worked in the computer industry. Linda Vista was a prized place to live; Katie understood this. It was a fairly new town that had grown up with the industry, and it had good schools and parks and shopping centers and curving streets of ranch style houses that showed that the families who lived in them were comfortably off. There were never houses for sale in Linda Vista. If a family moved, the house was sold before anyone ever had a chance to put a sign up. "Thank goodness we bought ours while you were still working," Dad used to say to Mom. "We could never swing it now."

Katie knew they were lucky—that she was lucky. She had her own room that looked out on the back garden where she had a bed of her own with flowers she especially liked blooming the year round—daffodils in spring, summer zinnias in all colors, chrysanthemums in fall (she picked her own for football games) and camellia bushes in winter against the redwood fence, where she could run out and pick a white, a pink, a deep red, any time to pin in her thick, light brown hair. "Gran loves flowers," Dad told her when he came back from the east. "You and she will have a lot in common."

It had still seemed all right then. When Katie was four and five, she had spent summers with her grandparents. She remembered how much she had loved her grandmother. It was Gran who read her the stories that were part of the good memories of being young and safe and warm on someone's lap, munching a cookie, thinking sleepily of bed but loving to stay and hear *The Gingerbread Man* or *Peter Rabbit* or *Alice in Wonderland*.

But then, at the family council, something happened inside Katie when Mom said to Dad (and Katie, too, she supposed), "John, you know we mustn't leave Gran alone here. Ever. It isn't just that her broken hip hasn't done all that well. . . ."

"I hope to goodness not," Dad said. "She can use that cane of hers and get around better than you or I any day."

"I know. But I'm talking about the way she'll feel. There's the shock, and even worse, there's the grief. It can take a toll. It's going to be a long while before she feels like herself again," Mom said. "I know if I were the one . . ."

"You? Come on, Nancy." Dad looked somehow shocked. Katie felt that way, too. Had Mom ever really thought about Dad dying? "I'm a mere kid of thirty-seven."

"As if I didn't know, darling." Mom leaned over on the couch and kissed him. "I wasn't thinking of you. I have a feeling it's just something I understand—something women know. Even Katie . . ."

The sentence trailed off, and Katie knew she was supposed to chime in. But the truth was, she didn't understand what Mom was talking about. The only grief she could remember was when Beaut, her dog, had had puppies and one of them died. She had cried herself to sleep for three nights and still believed that only she knew how Beaut herself mourned the loss.

But Mom was talking again now. "As I see it, we've got to count on Katie to help. When I have to be at the Senior Center to give my art classes, or the times when you or I are away at nights, well, Katie will surely need to be here."

"I think you're right," Dad said. "You usually are, Nancy." He hugged her. "So, with your help, we can work it out, Katie. Got that?" He turned to Katie and hugged her, too.

"You mean she's so old someone has to hang around and watch her?" Katie knew her words were all wrong, but she said them anyway. "You mean I can't even go out of the house if you two aren't here?"

Mom and Dad looked at each other and then at Katie. "Goodness, Katie," her mother finally said, "we aren't out on the town that often, are we?"

Desperately Katie looked at her feet—and saw her dog. "Why can't Beauty take care of Gran?" she said then, and it seemed a reasonable enough suggestion. They were always telling Beaut to take care of the house when the three of them took off. But of course, it wasn't a good suggestion at all. The dead silence told her that.

"Don't you love your grandmother?" Dad finally asked sternly.

It was the worst question anyone could have asked. Fortunately Mom knew it. "That's really not a fair question, John. Why, Katie hasn't seen Gran for ten years."

"Maybe. But thinking about herself first before her own grandmother doesn't make me very proud of the job you and I have done. And that's the truth!" Dad tended to get mad easily, but it still hurt when he walked out of the room.

"I'm sorry, Mom," Katie said. "Please. Honest, it's just that I . . . oh, I don't know. I just kind of thought this year I was going to have a lot of fun."

"There, dear, you'll have fun. This isn't some disaster. . . ."

"But, Mom," Katie interrupted, "no one else has a grandmother living with them! You know that."

"Maybe so. And maybe that's their misfortune," Mom said.

"But grandmothers around here aren't old," Katie pushed on. "I mean, Terri has a grandmother. She lives in a condominium over in Los Altos. She's got this nifty blond hair in little curls all over her head, and she wears high-heeled boots and takes cruises and drives Terri to dancing class in a terrific little red convertible. You ought to see her!"

"Heavens," Mom said, raising her eyebrows, "I guess I sure ought to."

"And Pam's grandmother—well, she lives in that retirement place across the bay. She has her own cottage. She plays golf every day, and Pam calls her Irene."

Dad came back into the room just then. "Calls her Irene, you say? Calls her grandmother Irene." He was still cross, that was clear. He began to sing sarcastically, "Goodnight, Irene, goodnight . . . goodnight, Irene . . ."

"Oh, stop, John," Mom said.

"I won't stop. Why should some teenage kid think she can call her grandmother by her first name?"

"Maybe her grandmother likes it that way," Mom said mildly.

"And if mine does, I'll never know," Katie said suddenly to her father. "Because I don't even know Gran's first name. So there!"

The room became very still. Dad didn't walk out. Mom didn't say anything. Beaut sat like a statue. And Katie felt grim. Finally Dad sighed, and his voice was low when he spoke. "Your grandmother's first name, Katie, is Nora. Funny you should ask. It was almost yours. Remember, Nancy? We almost . . ."

"I know, we almost named her Nora. It's a lovely name."

Katie couldn't stand feeling mean—*being* mean —any longer. Impulsively she got up and went to her father and put her arms around him. "Mom's

right, Dad," she said. "It's a very pretty name.
And I'm sorry. Honest."

"Me, too, hon," he said. "Let's all just do the
best we can and be thankful Gran can be with us.
Okay?"

Beaut leaned against their legs, wagging her tail.

2

Now it was Monday. Mom had gone to teach her art class at the Senior Center, and Katie was babysitting. Why Gran couldn't go and learn art too was a question Katie hadn't dared to ask. Ever since that terrible night when she had somehow said everything wrong to her parents and when Dad had somehow hurt her, too, she'd tried to do the right thing. When Gran had arrived Friday afternoon, she had even offered her own room "because it looks out on the flowers," she'd said, "and Dad says you like flowers, Gran."

Of course, Gran had refused. After all, they'd fixed up the larger guest room down the short hall from Katie especially for Gran, with a new yellow down quilt and curtains to match and a little velvet lounge chair with a footstool whose top lifted up to reveal a sewing box. And Mom's favorite silver-framed picture of Dad when he graduated from Cal was right there on top of the heavy, old mahogany bureau Katie's grandparents had given their son when he got married.

It had been easy enough to call her grandmother Gran, because like it or not, she looked like an old lady. She was thin and had white hair drawn back in a bun. If she'd ever been to a beauty shop, it must have been years ago. And she walked with a cane. The fact that the cane had a marvelous lion's head on it didn't negate the fact that without it Gran was in danger of falling. Her clothes consisted mostly of flowered prints. They were pretty dresses, but they were shapeless, and her lace slip showed underneath, which would have been okay except that Gran also wore tennis shoes—or worse, sometimes jogging shoes—with knee-length stockings that showed her bare knees when she sat down and crossed her legs.

"Look at that," Gran had said that first Saturday. "You and I have shoes just alike."

They weren't just alike at all. Gran had some kind of cheap, fake jogging shoes that must have come from a cut-rate drug store, while Katie had the most expensive running shoes money could buy—her own and the extra that had been her Easter present. Of course, you couldn't say that, and so she'd laughed and assured Gran that their shoes were twins for sure, and the awful truth (which she couldn't say either but knew with a fierce certainty) was that she, Katie Marshall, was ashamed of her grandmother.

Now the Monday afternoon was passing, and she sat with Gran in the living room looking out the window when she could. For DeeDee had promised she'd come by the minute school was over. Katie was dying to tell her friend about standing face to face with Brian Foster. She could see DeeDee's wide eyes, hear her breathe, "Fabulous!" Katie would describe the way he'd pulled her blue ribbon and taken her by the hand and smiled at her, and "wait till you hear this, DeeDee—he called me Kate!"

No one ever called Katie Marshall Kate—except once in a great while her father, and that was when he was cross and wanted her to do what he used to call "sit up and take notice." This was not at all the way Brian had said it. He'd just said "Kate"; how could she describe it? Kate, as if she were a totally wonderful person—a woman, someone he liked— and it all came out like the most natural thing in the world. Kate. Katie was off in a dream world, hearing the way the word sounded from Brian Foster's smiling lips, over and over. Kate.

"Looking for someone, Katie?" Gran's voice came then, bringing her back to reality with a brutal crash. If Brian had wanted even for a moment to talk to her more, to know her better, the impulse must have passed in a flash when he saw her climb into the little station wagon with the old woman who cried, "Katie-doll!"

But she was determined to do what was right— the best she could, just as Dad had said. "My friend DeeDee's coming over, Gran," she said. "You'll like her. We've been friends since we were five years old. She's sort of short and maybe a little chubby and she wears glasses, neat ones," she added, "and she and I just joined the Joggers Club."

"That sounds like a good place to lose some weight, meet some nice boys and have some good times," Gran said. She got up, using her cane, and went into the kitchen. For a plate of cookies, Katie knew—and Beaut knew, too, for she followed as close as she could without knocking Gran over. Katie could hear that she was rewarded. "Sit, Beauty dear," Gran's voice came, and then there was a little bark and then, "Good woofing, Beauty. Here you go." Crunch. Beaut had her cookie.

DeeDee arrived, and then Mom, who said right away, "You two go along on your afternoon run. Just be back in time to help with dinner, Katie."

Katie and DeeDee took off with Beaut on a leash and ran their prescribed number of blocks without saying much. If you were running well, you couldn't be telling your best friend everything that had happened. Katie wished they were off in the hills, running in Woodlands Park where the older kids went, where you could stop once in a while and sit in the shade and talk all you wanted to. But she was forbidden by her parents, and Dee-Dee by hers, to run anywhere else but in the bike paths around the few blocks near their homes. In a way they both understood that running in the nearby hills on trails and horse paths that went into deep woods and out onto high meadow slopes was considered dangerous for young girls, even those who ran in pairs. Still, other girls were at least allowed to run in Woodlands, the twenty-five-hundred-acre community park with gates that were opened and closed morning and night.

Katie always said, "Why can't we go if I take Beaut? No one would dare come near us."

"For one thing, you haven't got transportation up there," Dad always said, and that was that.

So they ran around the familiar blocks, past the little neighborhood park, past DeeDee's house, past Brian's, too, on Arlington Circle, where DeeDee managed to whistle and giggle and raise her eyebrows and wink—all in the seconds it took to go by the long, low gray house with the country mailbox where wrought-iron letters spelled out FOSTER.

At the end of the line, the corner of Oak and Meadow, they stopped and panted for a minute and then went into everyone's favorite store: Mel's Stop and Shop, open twenty-four hours a day, but probably doing its best business between four and six in the afternoon when half of Linda Vista High always managed to show up for soda and sour cream potato chips.

DeeDee drank down a whole diet coke. "Is your grandmother really so awful?" she asked.

"I guess not. No, she's not," Katie said. She slid down onto the floor of the concrete parking lot, her back to the wall, and idly untied one of her shoelaces. She noticed DeeDee's laces. They were white with the words *AWESOME* and *FANTASTIC* printed over and over in pink and red. "Those are neat laces, DeeDee," she said, "really wild." Then she sighed. "As for Gran, she's okay. I guess."

"What do you mean, 'I guess?'" DeeDee asked.

"Well, I mean for one thing, she keeps asking me what I want to be."

"Gee, you don't mean it!" DeeDee said, giggling. "I thought that question went out with *Leave it to Beaver.*"

"So what am I supposed to say? I don't know what I want to be!"

"Your mother was a teacher," DeeDee ventured.

"Sure, but it's not so easy to get a job teaching any more. Besides," Katie added, "I don't necessarily want to be whatever Mom was."

DeeDee nodded understandingly. "I know what you mean. Take my mom. She likes being a hospital dietitian just fine. But me, well, who knows?"

The two girls might have gone on for some time exploring their futures in this relaxed sort of way if they hadn't been interrupted by the arrival of an old maroon-colored Mustang convertible that pulled into the parking lot, top down, loaded with laughing boys and girls whose shouts drowned out all conversation. They were seniors, one and all, and acting, as usual, as if they owned the place. Katie and DeeDee shrank back against their wall and watched, just as sophomores were supposed to do. And the fact that Katie recognized that Mustang—didn't everyone in town?—only made her try harder to become invisible.

"Okay, everybody out. End of the line!" It was Brian Foster's voice, and if he'd looked down past the wheel of his car instead of throwing his head back and laughing along with his passengers, he'd have looked straight into Katie's eyes. He pushed the car door open, and she could see he had on his warm-up suit, an old, gray, baggy school one. "LVHS," it would say on the back of the sweat shirt, and their school mascot, that crazy roadrunner, would be imprinted there. Brian was the track star who brought four state championships home to Linda Vista as a junior last year and led the school's cross-country team to victory, too. The rumor was that he was going to Stanford next year, unless Yale and Pomona could do some last-minute persuading.

"Come on," he urged his gang. "Out! I've got to get onto the track and do twenty laps or get it from Coach."

Three girls and a boy got out. They were all wearing elaborate running clothes. The last girl had on some flimsy orchid shorts and a matching striped shirt that clung to her shapely figure. Deliberately she climbed out the other side of the car, right over Brian Foster, and Katie saw that even her British running shoes were orchid-colored. As she slid over the closed door, the girl patted him on the head in a familiar sort of way and said loudly, "Later, Brio. Later."

Brian Foster didn't seem to mind at all. He just grinned and waved as he did a neat U-turn and drove off.

"Look at those jerks," DeeDee muttered to Katie. "Wearing headbands, carrying *Runner Magazine* tote bags and loaded with eye shadow! Yuk! How phony can you get?"

"Dumb, all right," Katie said.

"Dumb? Listen," DeeDee said, "those girls

haven't run a lap since they were into Play-Doh—which they still are!"

Katie couldn't help giggling.

"I mean," DeeDee went on, "their idea of a fun run is probably three blocks to the pizza parlor chased all the way by the LV track team!"

And with this remark Katie's giggles turned to outright laughter.

"Hey, someone think something's funny?" a voice said. The girl in the orchid outfit came over Katie's way. "Something funny?" she repeated.

"You mean me?" Katie said. She recognized the girl, she was the one Brian Foster had tossed his sweater to that morning. She was a member of the group Katie and her friends called the Crumb Bunch. Seniors. Girls with privileges and dates and cars and makeup and neat clothes. Her name was Margo Gilman.

"I sure do mean you, kiddo." Margo moved toward Katie. It was a mistake. Beaut, disregarding her leash, rose and snarled and put herself between the two girls.

Margo looked scared for a moment and drew back, but then said, "This your dog? Well, call it off, soph. And I'm not just kidding!"

"Down, Beaut, down!" Katie wasn't kidding either. Beaut could be fierce when she wanted to be, and she clearly didn't like Margo Gilman.

Tugging on the leash, Katie managed to pull the dog to a sitting position. "Good dog, Beaut," she said. "Good dog."

Now Margo acted as if there had been no scare ever in her voice. "Beaut?" she said. "Your dog's name is Beaut? That mutt?"

"She's a Lab," Katie said, gritting her teeth.

"That dog—a Lab?" Margo's voice was scornful. "I never saw a black Lab with feathers on her legs. Sort of gray feathers at that," she added, and everyone laughed.

"She's a Lab," Katie persisted stubbornly. "Her mother was a Lab, and her name is Black Beauty."

"Black Beauty!" Margo echoed. "How quaint. Get that, friends. This mutt's name, mixed pedigree, gray hairs and all, is Black Beauty."

Her gang laughed again. Katie said nothing. DeeDee glared.

"Besides," Margo went on, "Black Beauty was a horse." She paused. "In case you didn't know."

"I know," Katie said.

"And a thoroughbred."

"I know," Katie said again.

"And a male," Margo finished triumphantly. "Black Beauty was a male."

"I know all that," Katie said. And suddenly, like her dad, she was mad. "What am I supposed to do? Apologize? I was five years old when I got Beaut. She was black and she was a beauty and my grandmother had just read me the story. . . ."

"Your grandmother?" interrupted Margo Gilman. There was real laughter now.

"That's right, all of you guys, my grandmother! And to me, this dog is beautiful. She's ten years old—that's seventy for dogs—and she's still my black beauty!"

Beaut heard her name and barked and wagged her tail and licked Katie's face, and Katie could hear Margo in the background, "Disgusting! Letting some old dog lick your face!"

The gang went inside the store. Katie and Dee-Dee, with Beaut trailing, took off for home.

Home, Katie thought, and Gran. She'd said the magic word *grandmother*, and everyone had laughed, and if he'd been there, Brian Foster would probably have laughed, too. But he hadn't been there. He'd wheeled up and then driven off again without even saying hello, much less "Hello, Kate," and some other girl had touched him and called him Brio. Katie felt terrible.

"Why didn't Beauty bite that old bag Margo Gilman?" DeeDee said, panting as she worked to keep up with Katie. "I mean, I wish Patch had been there. She'd have killed her!" Patch was DeeDee's calico kitten, orange and white and gray with a big black spot over one eye, a true pirate rightly named Patch and a pretty feisty number at that.

And suddenly, as they rounded the corner of the park on the last block before Ivy Lane, Katie began to laugh. She had to. The thought of little Patch attacking Margo Gilman with her snooty look and silky hair in that silly purple headband was just too much.

"I vote we team up Beaut and Patch and sic them on the whole Crumb Bunch any time we see them," she shouted to DeeDee as they headed up her driveway. "We're not afraid of them. And that includes Brian Foster, too. Because he's one of them!"

3

One week later Katie was being reminded of that very remark about the gang and Brian Foster. A meeting of the Joggers Club was scheduled for 3:00 P.M. sharp in the home ec room at school. Katie had decided not to go, but she didn't like it when DeeDee accused her of being scared of the gang.

"Why not go? We're members, aren't we?" DeeDee had her pinned against her locker just outside their last class. "You said we shouldn't be afraid of them. Well, I know I'm not!" she said defiantly and began to walk off.

"Come on, DeeDee," Katie said, "I'm not afraid either. But what's the point of going? The club is run by the Crumb Bunch, you know that."

"You mean you don't want to help plan the homecoming float? Or even see Brian Foster?" DeeDee asked, still walking.

30

Katie went after DeeDee then, and together they wedged into the crowded home ec room. There must have been over thirty boys and girls inside. Running was a big sport with the teenagers in Linda Vista and with a good many of their parents, too. At LV High, track was almost as popular as football. Even the school mascot was a roadrunner. Of course, nothing would take the place of the traditional fall big game with Sunnyvale on Thanksgiving Day, but spring, with its week-long homecoming celebration before the final track meet of the season, seemed to become more special every year. For one thing, the whole town joined in. Merchants entered floats, too, and the parade wound through the five cordoned-off blocks of downtown before ending up at the high school. There everyone picnicked, and there were races all afternoon for every age, from sack races for kindergartners to a one-mile fun run for seniors.

The festivities culminated just before dark at the close of the school band concert. The entire track team, boys and girls both, trooped onto the field led by the cross-country runners and lined up in front of the bandstand. The coach took the microphone then and introduced each member of his team. Amid cheers, each was crowned with a small wreath by the newly elected homecoming queen, who had led the parade and would reign at the dance in the gym that night.

It was typical of the spirit of this event that every member of the team was crowned. There was a queen, yes, but there never was a king or any kind of winner singled out, no matter how much of a star one of the team members might be in a track meet

or how many records he might hold. This attitude
was the doing of one man, Coach Ken Miles. In
fact, the track coach at Linda Vista High was
mainly responsible for the kind of spirit that per-
vaded not only homecoming week but the entire
track program at LV.

Kenneth Mack Miles had been known, ever
since his college competition days, as Dusty.
Whenever some smart-alec said, "I suppose with a
name like Miles you *had* to run," he always answered, "Sure, and if I had a name like Byrd, I'd
have to fly," and that ended that. Dusty Miles
looked like what a member of the Crumb Bunch
once termed "your basic jock coach." He was tall
and at thirty-five still steel-thin and hard. He had a
tan, craggy face that looked pretty stern and scary
until he smiled, and he had a stiff, bristle crew cut,
a style so old-fashioned that he looked like a World
War II marine out of an old John Wayne movie.
But one of the charms of Coach Dusty Miles was
that his appearance completely hid the truth of the
man himself. As the Crumb Bunch member had
gone on to say, "But instead of your basic jock
coach, he's a real piece of cake."

Coach Miles wasn't exactly a piece of cake
either, as his teams could attest. He had standards
so high, you left high school without reaching them
and knew you'd spend the rest of your life trying.
And that's probably where the stern look came
from, and that made it all right, especially when
you knew the guy behind that look was just about
the most cheerful, friendliest man who ever put on
a coaching jacket and stepped in front of a high
school track team.

Dusty Miles cared about kids, not about winning. "The only records I'm interested in are P.R.'s," he'd say again and again. P.R. stood for "personal record"—your own best time at any distance. "So when you win big against yourself," the coach would say, "then let me know. I hand out ribbons for that kind of record." He did, too. He had blue ribbons imprinted in gold: "P.R.—1st Place—LVHS." The team members who came and claimed them treasured them ever after.

As to the winning, the wondrous result of Ken Miles's philosophy was that Linda Vista track teams won consistently year after year. The more he told them, "If you run for Miles, you run for fun," the more they won. When he said, "If you think you broke the pain barrier, don't tell me about it, because I don't even believe in it," faces lost their grim looks and bodies took off faster than ever.

It was this kind of attitude that led to the club at Linda Vista being called the Joggers Club instead of the Runners Club. Coach Miles was the group's sponsor, and he had vetoed the name Runners Club in the first five minutes of the first meeting. He knew just how much some of the young people there liked to assert their superiority over others. "Listen," one boy said, "we're not just dumb old joggers, fat and forty. I'll bet no one here takes over seven minutes to do a mile."

"Well, I'm not fat, and I've got a few years before I'm forty," the coach shot right back, "but I sure am a jogger." Everyone there knew that Dusty Miles had broken records in college, had run the Pikes Peak Marathon and the Mount Washington and then had done the Boston Marathon twice, finishing in the top ten both times. He also ran the 7.5-mile Bay to Breakers every May right in San Francisco and never finished lower than fourth place. It seemed a little strange to hear him refer to himself as a jogger.

He laid it on the line. "Let me tell you something, all of you. When I do a six-minute mile, I'm just jogging. And so are most of you. So get that straight. On the other hand, some folks can be doing a twelve-minute mile and be running their hearts out, not jogging at all. Saying anyone who takes over seven minutes to do a mile is just jogging is phony as all get-out. I mean it. What we want with this club is for everyone who loves running to get off their duffs and get the heck out here and join up! And that means guys, gals, freshmen, seniors—and faculty, too." He paused and fixed them with one of his fierce looks. "Right?" he challenged.

"Right!" they all hollered. And the club became the Joggers Club then and there. It may have been the first such club in a California high school. It was surely the biggest, and it had as many girl members as boys. Some were on the girls' track team, but most were just recreational runners. DeeDee claimed they joined the club just to get into fancy shorts and show off their legs and hope the track team was watching. But that wasn't quite fair. A lot of them loved running. Certainly Katie did. Dusty Miles had them organized into intramural teams, and she liked the fun of that mild competition.

Katie knew the coach used the intramural program to recruit serious runners for his teams.

When he spotted girls who looked promising, he'd time their laps and congratulate them and try to persuade them to get into his weekly training program. He could make it sound fascinating. "Endurance first, then strength and last of all, speed," he'd tell them. "That's what we're after. So get out there and run every day and don't put a stopwatch on yourself for at least six weeks. Speed will come, and without doing any wind-sprints either."

Wind-sprints were forced, short-speed runs. They were purposely brutal; they could make runners be sick or even collapse. Some coaches loved them. "They build wind," they'd say, "shape a man up." But Dusty Miles never allowed them.

Katie herself ran because she loved it—the feel of wind against her face, the way her head seemed to float, the sense of freedom as her legs took her on and on. When Katie ran, she felt clean and strong and clear about everything. Sometimes, for instance, a day could be one P.W. after another. P.W. was your "personal worst" in running, but Katie and DeeDee used it to stand for all disasters of any kind. When she had a day like this, Katie knew that no matter how bad things seemed, they would all fall away—worry, anger, whatever it was—when she ran.

There was a motto hanging in Coach Miles's tiny office in the gym. "You can't run and feel sorry for yourself," it said. Katie knew this was true, and for her, it was reward enough for running. She had never entered any real competition beyond some family fun runs, and even they weren't competition since the very essence of fun runs was not having any speed limits or any winners. Nevertheless Katie sensed that she was something of a natural runner. She knew there were reserves in her that she had never used, never let out. Running four laps for a 5:28 mile was just not hard for her when she exerted herself even a little.

Thus Katie shouldn't have been surprised in her freshman year when Coach Miles had approached her to talk about his training program and urge her to sign up for running spring quarter. Maybe she wasn't surprised, but she had felt shy about it and somehow resistant, too. She knew her dad would like her to be on the track team; he was a big admirer of Dusty Miles. If she'd been a boy, he'd probably have signed her up himself. But Katie had been quite sure she didn't want to commit herself to running every day and getting all excited about beating someone.

As for the coach, even if he said he didn't care who won, Katie knew he did care in some way, and she knew that if you put yourself in his hands, you'd begin to care, too. You'd want to do well, if not to win a medal, well then, just to win his approval. When he began to watch her doing laps that spring and told her once, "You could go far running, Katie," she blushed with pleasure. And when he added, grinning, "You're built just right for it," she really blushed, and this was partly because Brian Foster, who didn't even know who she was, was standing right there.

In her sophomore year Katie had signed up for running every quarter, though she had not gone out for the track team. Still she knew she was taking her running more seriously. For one thing, she now ran every day seven days a week, and furthermore, she felt a real need to do it. She found that it was still fun; in fact, her pleasure seemed to have increased. But some important part of her did not yet want to race. Perhaps Coach Miles understood this, because he didn't press her, and she was grateful to him for that.

Now today in the crowded Home Ec room where the Joggers Club was meeting, Katie saw Coach Miles come in quietly and stand by the door. He caught her eye, and she waved. He winked and nodded, and she felt good.

"Okay, everyone, pipe down!" It was Brian Foster's voice, and Katie, like the rest, turned dutifully in his direction. He was sitting casually on the edge of one of the counters by a kitchen sink, holding up one hand. "Coach is here," he said, "so let's get going."

"Come on, now," Ken Miles protested. "You don't need me."

"No, but we want you," one of the girls called out. "Oh, how we want you!" Everyone laughed.

"The first order of business," Brian said, "is to find a place to meet. Mrs. Anderson is a doll to let us crowd in here, but we need a place to spread out."

"Hear, hear!" the group cried.

"So if you can offer your home, say so." Some hands went up. "No, not now. Think it over. Maybe your mom doesn't like to make giant chocolate chip cookies." There was more laughter. Katie, still puzzled by Brian Foster, still cross with him, didn't join in, though some part of her couldn't help admiring the ease he showed in front of people. *Thinks he's so great,* she thought, and at the same time she found herself thinking helplessly, *Right, Katie, he's great.*

Brian went on. "I'll call for volunteers at the end of the meeting. The second order of business is electing a president, because I've just been holding the fort since Sue Morse moved, you know. And the third and most important item on the agenda is getting an all-time great idea for the Joggers Club float for homecoming."

"Hear, hear!" they shouted.

"Okay, nominations are in order for president of California's number-one high school joggers club."

"We're number one!" they shouted, and then in the din someone called out the name of Sam O'Neill, a junior boy DeeDee liked.

Sam declined the nomination. "I'm up at four every morning, guys. I'm not fit to be president of anything. In fact," he grinned, "you're lucky I'm here. I'm usually sacked out this time any afternoon trying to get ready to run some more."

Then someone nominated Lisa Scott, one of the senior gang of girls, and right away Margo Gilman said loudly, "I move the nominations be closed."

What happened next was hard later for Katie to recall. But she did remember DeeDee shouting, "That's not fair! I nominate Katie Marshall here and now!"

There was a lot of noise and some clapping and then one of the Crumb Bunch girls shouted, "This is ridiculous, Brian. There's a motion before the house. . . ."

"I didn't hear a second," Sam O'Neill put in cheerfully.

"And besides," the girl went on heatedly, "Katie Marshall's only a sophomore. You can't have a sophomore for president!"

"And why can't you?" There was DeeDee again, standing right up to her. "If it's in the bylaws, you'll have to show me!" Just like Patch, Katie thought. It was really kind of wonderful.

The two girls argued back and forth, and supporters shouted encouragement until finally Brian Foster got up on the table where he'd been sitting and motioned for attention. "Quiet, all of you." He didn't even have to wave his hands or shout. "Now listen, what are we arguing about, for Pete's sake? As far as I am concerned a sixth-grader could run for president and, if elected, could serve. So let's cool it and move on. We've got two nominations—Lisa Scott and Katie Marshall." So, she thought, I'm Katie after all to Brian Foster.

"Stand up, you two, wherever you are," he said. He looked around, and Lisa, who was right there beside the table, climbed up beside him. He grinned, took her hand and raised it high in the air. "And now in this corner," he said, holding up his other hand, "oops, where is she?"

People laughed and began to push Katie forward. "Aha," he said, seeing her at last, "there she is, Miss America!" He reached a hand down. "Right here by me, Kate," he said not loudly at all as he pulled her up close to him—and she was standing there, Kate after all, and she felt wonderful. He kept her hand and raised it high—Lisa's, too, on the other side of him—and the clapping and cheers came all over again.

Why she was elected Katie would never know, unless others besides herself and DeeDee were fed up with the senior girls. DeeDee said later, "You were elected because you run like a deer and anyway, you're the prettiest sophomore at Linda Vista High and the smartest, too!" But that was just a best friend's loyalty.

As to the float, that never got settled. The theme this year was "America the Beautiful."

"Plenty of leeway," Brian pointed out. "We can do anything."

"Sure," Margo said, "but we're so late getting started that the good ideas are already taken. All the clubs are latching onto nostalgia. The Math Club has even gotten hold of a covered wagon some place and that Lani Sears is making herself a Mother Hubbard costume to wear. And no wonder, it might even cover her up!"

Everyone laughed. "But this is serious," Sam said. "Margo's right. The best deals have already been lined up: covered wagon, Spirit of Seventy-six, the San Francisco Bay Bridge. And the Dance Club is going to have flappers from the twenties doing the Charleston."

"Maybe the truck driver will stop suddenly and they'll fall down," someone said, and they broke up laughing again, though it really wasn't very funny.

The truth was, no one had a good idea. "The French Club is going to show Nouvelle Cuisine—American Style. Mrs. Anderson is going to help them. Maybe we could have cowboys making flap-jacks."

"Aw, forget it!" someone shouted. "What we need to do is go home and think. And come up with an idea at our next meeting. There's still time."

"Okay," Brian said, "that settles it. And we'd better make the next meeting in two weeks. No later. Who volunteers?"

"Katie does." Incredibly the voice was DeeDee's. "Katie's the new president, so she might as well have the next meeting."

Brian jumped off the counter where he'd been for most of the meeting and pulled Lisa Scott after him. "All right," he said, looking up at Katie, "it's all yours, madam president."

And there she was, standing alone. What could she do? Somehow her voice came out. "You're all welcome to my house, 45 Ivy Lane, two weeks from today. Three-fifteen. On the dot. Giant chocolate chips, for sure. Two for everyone with a neat idea for the float!"

And then it was all over. Everyone was hurrying out of the crowded Home Ec room. She looked around. Brian had disappeared. So had Margo and Lisa and the whole senior gang—all together, off to the hills in someone's car, no doubt, leaving the nobodies, the DeeDees and Katies, behind. That's just the way it was.

Walking home with DeeDee, Katie gave in to her mixed feelings. She was happy and mad at the same time, triumphant and yet hurt, too. The Joggers Club had elected her president, but what difference did that make? Brian Foster had smiled at her in a special way and called her Kate, but what difference did that make either? Not sure what, exactly, she would say if she opened her mouth, she was glad when Sam O'Neill suddenly appeared and walked along with them. Although *walked* was not quite the word for the way Sam accompanied them. He jogged alongside, turned around when he got ahead and ran back, then circled them, jumping little hedges along the way and snapping his fingers as if he were listening to a favorite rock tune.

Maybe he was. As he came past DeeDee for the third time, he called out, "Care to dance, miss?"

The girls laughed. "Honestly, Sam O'Neill," DeeDee said, "don't you ever stand still?"

"Nope," he called back over his shoulder, "only when I sleep." Then suddenly he dropped onto a lawn and let them catch up. "Which I may do right now," he said, lying back. The lawn just happened to be the front yard of DeeDee's house.

And there he lay, stretched out a mile, it seemed, because Sam was so lanky that he looked even taller than his six feet. "When I get to be a senior, I'm going to fill out," he used to say, "and that's a direct quote from my mother." He had on faded jeans cut-offs, the oldest running shoes in Linda Vista and a baggy T-shirt that read, "I Love New York."

Katie and DeeDee folded onto the grass beside him, dropping backpacks off their shoulders. "Hey, anyone know the people who live here?" Sam asked innocently. "We're trespassing, you know."

DeeDee giggled. "Ogres live here," she said.

"Fierce ones. They'll run us off with huge clubs if they catch us."

"Ugh," Sam groaned, "and me too tired to move." He closed his eyes. "Just leave me here, ladies, if they come. Save yourselves."

The three of them sat there for a while, Sam "sleeping," DeeDee selecting special grass blades and chewing them, Katie suddenly relaxed and peaceful. What was there about Sam, anyway? He was just so easy to be with. You didn't even feel as if you had to say anything if you didn't want to. Maybe that's what having a brother would have been like, Katie thought. Anyway, it was not like being with other boys—like Brian, say, where you always had to worry about what you were saying, about what he thought of you, about what other girls were thinking of you. With Sam and DeeDee it wasn't that way.

Katie picked a daisy from the lawn border and laid it on Sam's chest. "Do you really love New York?"

"Who, me?" he said, opening one eye. He shrugged. "I'll have to check it out some day. I've never been there. What I love is California—and DeeDee Ross and Katie Marshall and all sophomore girls." He laughed. "But a guy has to take his threads where he can get them. Actually my grandparents brought me this T-shirt when they visited last summer. Hey," he said, sitting up suddenly, "you've got a neat grandmother, Katie."

Panic set in. Neat grandmother? How did Sam O'Neill even know there was a grandmother at her house? She thought that dark secret was known at

Linda Vista High only by herself and DeeDee Ross. That's the way she'd tried to keep it. And DeeDee had promised not to tell. Had that Brian Foster guessed who it was calling out "Katie-doll" from the car window that one afternoon when he was so nice to her? Or had DeeDee told Sam? Well, no, she wouldn't—DeeDee *wouldn't*.

"How would you know I have a grandmother?" she burst out at Sam.

"Look, doesn't everybody?" Sam said. Then he added, "You're just lucky."

"Lucky?" Katie's voice was heavy with sarcasm, but Sam ignored it.

"Sure, I mean, heck, there she is living with you," he said.

Something broke in Katie, and she turned on her friend. "Okay, DeeDee Ross, you promised, but you told anyway. Didn't you? Admit it!"

DeeDee looked puzzled, then angry. "What are you talking about? You sound weird, Katie, I mean really weird. I haven't told Sam anything! But if I had, what's the big deal? Grandmothers aren't some sort of outcasts, are they?"

"They certainly aren't," Sam broke in. "Ever see one in Poker Flats?" Trust Sam, always trying to make things go right by saying something funny. But DeeDee and Katie were having none of it.

"She thinks I ratted on her, Sam," DeeDee said hotly. "For gosh sakes, why would I do that?"

"Well, someone told, because Sam has never met my grandmother," Katie shot back.

"Hey, hold on, you two," Sam said. "I have so met your grandmother, Katie."

This stopped both girls, and they listened. "You

don't think I get up at four in the morning and run, run, run for the sheer joy of running, do you? Listen, I run my hour, and then I hit the old paper route. That's right," he said cheerfully. "I'm the oldest living paperboy in captivity. Sixteen years old and I'm still delivering the old San Francisco *Chronicle* on doorsteps."

Katie remembered then. Sam's mother was a widow. She had a good job as the secretary in the English department at the nearby junior college. But there were five O'Neill kids, all of them worked at something. Sam was the oldest, and as to the paper route, he was being modest. Katie knew that he was the manager for six routes, yet still kept up his own. He wanted to go to college—U.C. Berkeley—to study geology. "If you have to go for a Ph.D.," he used to say, "you'd better start a bank account in the second grade."

He probably has a big one by now, Katie thought, and DeeDee's lucky to have someone like Sam fall for her. As to Gran, though . . . "Okay, Sam," Katie said, "so you deliver the *Chronicle* to Ivy Lane. You're not saying you had a formal introduction there some morning, are you? Because we aren't even up at that hour."

"Maybe you aren't," Sam said, "but your grandmother sure is."

Katie couldn't believe it. Gran's room was just down the hall from hers. They shared a bathroom. Mom and Dad's master bedroom suite was way off at the other end of the house. If Gran got up early, she, Katie, would certainly know it. For one thing, Gran was noisy: She had that cane, and she sort of talked to herself, too. That was one of the things that embarrassed Katie about her. No, she wasn't up and about at 5:00 A.M. Still, what was Sam saying?

"I used to pass your house and hit the front walk with my paper right by the hawthorn bush without a blink from anyone, even your dog. Old Beaut knows me. She never made a sound."

How did Sam know Beauty's name? Sam caught Katie's puzzled look. "Paper boys—or excuse me, girls, paper *persons,* because it's true some of my best carriers are girls now—well, we always learn the names of every dog on the route. Ever face a Doberman at six in the morning on Mariposa Way and wonder if you'd ever make it back out to Altos Avenue again? Hey, you've got to be able to say, 'Good morning, Rusty—good dog—good old Rusty.'"

Fascinated, the girls listened to Sam. "But one morning not long ago, Katie, this neat lady was sitting on your porch—well, I suppose in California we call it a front patio, but I'll bet she calls it a porch. Anyway, she said, 'Hi, young fellow.'"

Oh, no! "Young fellow?" How could Gran . . .

"So," Sam was going on, "I rode right up the driveway and deposited the paper in her lap, and ever since, we've been best friends. Once she even gave me an old-fashioned cake doughnut."

Katie remembered; Sam was right. Gran *had* gotten up at least once. There had been a plate of fresh homemade doughnuts on the breakfast table.

Sam stood up. "Enough, ladies. I must be off for the great late afternoon O'Neill effort in behalf of the track team of Linda Vista High." He started to go, then stopped. "See you tomorrow, Katie. I promised your grandmother. And maybe you, too, DeeDee, if you have the smarts to get yourself over to forty-five Ivy Lane."

And he was off, loping down the winding street like an antelope, and when he came to a manhole covered by a sawhorse with a red flag tied to it, he went over in a style that would have won the low hurdles on any track anywhere.

Katie wondered about the casual mention of tomorrow at 45 Ivy Lane, but all she said was, "Sam's nice, DeeDee."

DeeDee nodded in a dreamy kind of fashion. "Katie, listen. Is it hard to kiss—I mean really kiss—with glasses?"

Katie had to laugh. "You nut. How would I know? I haven't got glasses. And I haven't ever 'really kissed,' as you put it." Then she remembered Sam's parting words. "What did Sam mean about seeing me tomorrow? And you? Have we three got a date or something?"

"Not me," DeeDee said. "But if Sam says come on by, I'll come." She stood and started up her walk.

"But DeeDee, what about my grandmother? What did Sam mean?"

"How would I know?" DeeDee said, then added, "Listen, you've got some kind of thing about your grandmother, Katie Marshall. What's supposed to be the matter with her, anyway?"

"She says 'good grief' all the time," Katie burst out.

"Yeah, and so does Charlie Brown," DeeDee said. "Is that all?"

"Of course it's not all!" Katie said indignantly.

"There are a thousand things. I mean, the worst—maybe the worst—is that she calls me Katie-doll all the time. I mean it. It's gross."

"Katie-doll," DeeDee repeated, and then said it again. "Gee, I kind of like it."

"You would!" Katie said. "You haven't heard the rest, though. When I was little, really little, probably a baby or something, she used to sort of sing to me. Oh, I don't know, it was sort of a song she made up, I guess. For when she was rocking me. It went, 'Katie-doll, Katie-did, up she went and down she slid.'" Katie stopped, then went on with an effort. "You've heard of katydids; they're kind of like crickets. You know, they sing. . . ."

Her voice trailed off in embarrassment. She couldn't even look at DeeDee.

"I think that's wonderful," DeeDee said softly. "It was a lullaby. Don't you see? And she made it up specially for you. I'll bet you loved it."

"Maybe I did," Katie admitted. "But that was years and years and years ago! How would you like to be fifteen and right in front of all your friends have someone call you DeeDee-doll?"

"I wouldn't," DeeDee said right away, beginning to laugh. "It would come out Didy-doll. And then how would I feel?"

It was no use. Katie had to laugh, too. "Darn you, DeeDee Ross. You're hopeless!"

DeeDee was at her front door now. It seemed to Katie that there were things she still wanted to tell her, to make her understand how it was with Gran. "Wait, DeeDee," she called. "I haven't told you everything."

"Uh-uh." DeeDee shook her head, already half-

way through the door. "You've told me enough. And what I think is maybe you're just making a great big problem where there isn't any—chalking up a real P.W."

"That's easy for you to say!" Katie yelled at DeeDee's disappearing back. "She's not your grandmother. You're not living with her!"

But DeeDee was gone.

4

Late that night Katie sat in her room by herself. She'd closed the door and said no, she didn't want to watch TV or make popcorn or anything else. She knew Mom and Dad thought she was being some kind of brat. What Gran thought, she couldn't imagine. And now it turned out that even DeeDee didn't understand how Katie felt.

Well, she had tried to like Gran. She *did* like her. After all, you had to like your own grandmother. But still, when someone dressed funny and talked out loud to herself and told the same story over and over and sometimes used your favorite shampoo . . .

"Mom, Gran uses my shampoo." Katie had tried one afternoon recently to talk to her mother about

Gran. "It's my favorite one, the special lemon—herbal stuff I have to send away for."

"Is that so terrible?" her mother said mildly. "You should be flattered. She must like it."

"She does. She says it makes her think of her own grandmother, of being a little girl again, whenever on earth that must have been!"

"Now, Katie . . ."

"But Mom, I have to wash my hair every single day. You know that!" Katie said passionately. "And if I get into the shower some morning and there isn't any shampoo, what am I supposed to do?"

Mom just looked at her for a minute and then said, "Well, as for your immediate morning beauty problem, I guess you could grab a bar of soap like lots of us do and go ahead and wash your glorious tresses. As for the long-range problem, I'd say you have what Dad calls some options—at least two. You can hide your precious bottle of Madam Sousa's lemon suds . . ."

"Mom!"

". . . and bring it out when you need it. Or you can send for three or four bottles at once so there'll be enough for both of you. Personally, I think I'd make the latter choice."

Katie thought she hated her mother at that moment. But then Mom went on, and the tone of her voice changed. "Katie, dear Katie. Don't make things so hard for yourself. I know it isn't easy sharing a bathroom with someone." She smiled. "I've been sharing one with your father for seventeen years now. You should see what he does with shampoo!"

She put her arm around Katie. "It's too bad you're an only child, I guess. You see, human beings are social creatures, Katie. We live with other human beings, and we like it that way. I mean," she amended, "we love it. It's worth it to learn to share. And Gran shares with you, doesn't she?"

Katie didn't answer. She felt too grim. Mom took her arm away and sighed as if she realized that getting philosophical hadn't helped that much. "Well, Katie," she said, "I've tried. And you mustn't think I don't understand. If I could only . . ." and then suddenly, she interrupted herself. "But I can," she said, "of course I can. Here's what we'll do. We'll share our problems. You and I. I'll tell you my own feelings once in a while. I've never done that before; I've just listened to yours. But you're old enough to understand now."

She smiled, and Katie felt a sudden rush of love flow through her.

"You mean you sometimes have feelings about Gran even?" Katie asked then, watching her mother intently.

"Of course I do, dear. How could I help it? Take sharing a kitchen, for instance. I get used to where I put a particular saucepan away, or how I fold the towels, or what bowl I use for mixing cake, and all at once there's someone else around who's been doing things a bit differently all her life in her own kitchen."

Mom paused, then went on. "But the point, Katie, is that I have to think how it is for her. You see, she isn't in her own kitchen any more—after years and years. So if once in a while she puts a pan in the wrong place after she washes it up . . ."

"Oh, but that's not all," Katie said. She had a fellow sympathizer now. "Sometimes she doesn't even get the pan clean. Haven't you noticed? The other day I had to take two spoons out of the drainer and do them over. . . ."

Katie broke off then because the expression that came over her mother's face stopped her. "Katie. Katie Marshall!" she exclaimed. "What is the matter with you? Haven't you heard anything I've said?" She shook her head. She was angry, and Mom didn't often get angry. "Listen to me now. Your grandmother gets her own breakfast and lunch and makes something nice for us in the kitchen whenever she has a chance. If you find a spoon not clean enough to suit you once in a while, well, young lady, you just wash it over again and keep quiet about it!"

That had ended that conversation. Katie was bitterly hurt. She'd trusted a grownup, her very own mother, and Mom hadn't understood. No one did. They were all against her—Dad, Mom, DeeDee, Sam. Even Beaut sided with Gran, come to think of it. Beauty had taken to lying down at Gran's feet and following her around and sitting like an angel whenever Gran said, "Sit!"

But no wonder, if every time someone said sit you got a peanut butter cookie or something just as good. Katie had even seen Gran cut a big piece of Jack cheese and divide it into little pieces and sit there and trade off with Beaut. "Beauty dear," she'd say, "here goes—one for you," and she'd pop a chunk into Beauty's soft, black and gray muzzle, "and one for me," and Beaut would look everlastingly happy.

Well, Katie thought late that night, there's no way out. In two weeks the Joggers Club would be meeting right there in her house, and there would be no way to ask Gran to please not put in an appearance. Mom wouldn't let her, Dad neither. Not them. When they heard about the meeting, they'd probably say, "Aren't you lucky, Katie? No one makes better giant chocolate chip cookies than your Gran!"

Oh, sure, right! And no one looks funnier in old lady's tennies than my Gran, too. Katie threw herself on her bed and put a pillow over her head and cried. What else could you do when no one was on your side and yet some part of you knew they were right? She fell asleep then, forgetting all about the immediate problem: tomorrow. She was to be alone all day with Gran while her parents went to a museum in San Francisco with Mom's art club. And Sam O'Neill was coming over because he'd promised her grandmother—something. What?

Katie always slept late on Saturday mornings. It was allowed. This Saturday the clock said 10:30 when she stirred, sighed, turned over, stirred again, thought she heard something, then almost went back to sleep. But she suddenly came awake after all. Because a chorus, a full glee club, it sounded like, began singing, "Put on your old gray bonnet with the blue ribbons on it. . . ."

She sat bolt upright. She must be dreaming.

". . . through the fields of zucchini we'll ride up to Sweeney. . . ."

No, she was not dreaming. Some sort of idiots were outside. By the time she got out of bed and over to the front living room window, the singers were on a third repeat of their crazy verse. And what she saw she couldn't believe. Out in the front yard were Gran and Sam and DeeDee, and Beauty, too, in what could only be termed a weird scene. Sam and DeeDee, with Beaut's help, were digging up the beautiful front lawn that Dad had worked so hard on with fertilizers and weed-killers, almost triumphing over the crab grass. And now, if Katie was seeing right, the whole area by the front walk had been turned over into hunks of dirt.

Pajamas and all, Katie flew out the door. "Hey, what do you guys think you're doing?" she shouted.

Gran, her cane in hand, said nothing. Beaut was still, too. DeeDee just looked surprised, and Sam pretended he didn't know what she meant. "We're doing what comes naturally," he called from the end of the driveway. "We're making the front yard into veggies."

Veggies! Were they totally out of their gourds?

Katie came down the walk and stood there with the three of them. It seemed Gran had hired Sam to turn up the lawn in favor of what was to be a gorgeous display of vegetables and flowers—the new thing in California living, evidently. And that explained why Sam was there. Explaining why DeeDee was there wasn't worth bothering about; it was obvious.

Sam broke the silence. "You see, Katie, if you

put sage in with the stock and snapdragons in with the bush beans and then some artichokes just back of the ivy . . ."

"And ruby chard with clumps of African daisies," DeeDee interrupted. "Wow! Can't you picture it?"

"You've been reading *Sunset Magazine,* I suppose," Katie said sulkily.

"*Uh-huh.* It's all from a book your grandmother has about what they call edible landscaping," DeeDee said. "And your parents think it's a great idea," she added pointedly.

"Here," Sam said, "have an edible," and he broke off three slender green stems of chive from a clump he was about to plant.

"Give them to DeeDee," Katie said frostily. "She loves to eat grass."

Of course she was behaving terribly, and of course she hated herself. Desperately Katie hoped someone would rescue her. Sam, as usual, tried. "Hey," he said, "are you always like this before breakfast?"

Gran seized on that. "That's it," she said. "Good grief, why didn't I think of it? The child hasn't had a bite to eat yet. Come along, you two," she said, shaking her cane in the direction of Sam and DeeDee, "let's all take a break while Katie has her breakfast. I've made some doughnuts. And Sam loves doughnuts, don't you, Sam?" She was moving up the walk slowly. "Coming, Beauty?" she called. "Coming, Katie-doll?"

Katie shuddered. But she moved. It was eleven o'clock by now. Maybe they could all get inside before the late morning jogging crowd came into view.

But she was not in time. And it wasn't the crowd, it was worse: Brian Foster turned a corner and came running by. By, but of course not quite by, because Sam hollered, "Hey, Brian, old buddy, over this way!"

So it was on that late April Saturday morning that Katie, through no doing of her own, found herself in her own front yard—or what was left of it—with Sam and DeeDee and Brian Foster. They all began to follow Gran and Beauty up the walk. Except Katie. She still stood rooted to the spot where she'd been when Brian peeled off without breaking his stride and ran past her straight into Sam O'Neill, who whooped and hollered, laughing as he went down into the new vegetable patch.

It was at this very moment that Katie realized she was standing there in front of them all—in front of Brian Foster—in her pajamas. If she could have sunk into the earth and pulled the clods of dirt over her, she would have. If she had anything to be thankful for, it was simply that the pajamas weren't her pink lace ones or the old, old ones with the teddy bears printed on them. They were, in fact, plain blue knit pajamas made like a jogging suit. And with luck, Brian might think that's what they were.

But Brian turned back just then as the rest went on inside and came right to the spot where she stood. He grinned at her. "Caught you in your p.j.'s, didn't I?" he said.

She blushed furiously, and Katie knew there was no way to hide a real Katie Marshall blush. It rose over her face like a bouquet of pink roses.

Brian laughed. "Hey," he said, "there's nothing to be embarrassed about. I wear blue pajamas myself." Suddenly he put his arm around her and held her—for just an instant—really close. His legs were bare, and hers, in the light pajamas, seemed almost bare, too. The feeling that came over her nearly stopped her breathing, and if he had not been holding her, she knew she surely would have fallen. As it was, she stumbled when he let go, and he caught her again, but this time he was careful to keep distance between them. Had he felt the way she felt? Was that why? Perhaps. He looked straight into her eyes then—deep—and his eyes were so blue, so piercing, as if there were something he wanted to know or something he must tell her with that look.

Then it was over. He took her hand firmly and began to walk with her to the door. She realized how much she liked having him take her hand, though he had held it only once before in her life. She wanted to say something, but she couldn't. And anyway, what would the words have been if she could have said them?

"Kate," he said. "Kate Marshall." That was all, but he tightened his hand on hers when he said it, and she thought this day had suddenly become the most perfect day in her whole life.

Later, in her room, Katie would try to figure out what went wrong, why everything changed so fast. It shouldn't have been like that. Because she and

Brian Foster, hand in hand, had gone inside the house at 45 Ivy Lane and followed the sound of laughter into the family room next to the kitchen. There Gran had lit a fire in the fireplace because the morning chill had not quite worn off, and there all of them sat around and ate doughnuts.

"For the afternoon break," Gran said, "we'll have root beer floats." And Katie hadn't minded for a minute that no one in Linda Vista drank root beer floats. When Gran said, "Wait till you taste my pure vanilla bean homemade ice cream with a little root beer over it," Katie had thought it sounded fine.

DeeDee sat beside Sam on the Indian rug, and once she winked at Katie, looking as if she were in some way happy for her, and that must have been because Brian still held her hand in his where they sat on the leather couch and because Beauty had brought her chin to rest exactly on top of Brian's bare knees and kept her eyes adoringly on his face.

Even when Gran said suddenly, "Katie-doll, could you bring me the old photo album from the top drawer in my bureau? Like a lamb. I'm just going to show these nice, young people what your father looked like at their age,"—even then Katie didn't mind. She just thought, "Oh, no," in a rather indulgent way and thought, too, "I wish I didn't have to take my hand from Brian's, even for a moment."

"I'll be right back," she said simply.

It was when she came back that things went wrong. Everything in the room had changed. Brian Foster was sitting over on the Indian rug by the fire with DeeDee and Sam. Mostly with DeeDee, it

seemed. Because he sat close to her, closer than
Sam did, and she was laughing up at him. The only
things that hadn't changed were Gran, who sat
cheerfully in her black rocking chair as if nothing
had happened, and Beauty, who, like the idiot she
was, still had her chin on Brian Foster's knees but
now had to lie down on the floor to achieve this
adoring position. And that was faithful dogs for
you, Katie thought.

"Hey, Katie, come on over here," Brian called.
So even her name was suddenly changed for him.
Had he ever called her Kate in that special way?
She wasn't sure. "I want you to look at DeeDee's
bracelet."

That's what he said, and incredibly he picked up
DeeDee's hand and held it toward Katie. Just as he
had held hers. Holding a girl's hand, any girl's, was
evidently just a casual gesture to Brian Foster.

Hurt and confused, Katie made herself go toward the three of them on the rug, dropping the
album on Gran's lap as she passed. She managed to
toss her head and try to smile as she stood there. "I
didn't know you had a new bracelet, DeeDee," she
said.

DeeDee giggled. "I don't. That is, I didn't.
Brian just gave it to me."

"Take a look, Katie." It was Sam speaking.

Then Brian. "Come on down here," he said, and
he reached for her hand.

Something—what?—made her pull back. "No,"
she said. She knew her voice sounded odd. But she
pushed on, standing all stiff and funny with Beauty's black bulk lying there between her and Brian.
"I mean, if you guys have something to show me,

do it. I—I have to catch some breakfast. And then study. I just haven't got all day."

Even to her, what she said sounded pretty dumb. But then DeeDee giggled and said, "Oh, come on, Katie, don't be such a lamebrain. Relax a little. You don't really have to study. You're so bright you don't have to study at all if you don't want to."

Why did this make Katie so mad? It was the kind of thing DeeDee was always saying to her and about her. But she felt all hot and angry, and before she knew it, she was treating her best friend like an enemy, saying things that made her cry minutes later in her room.

"Listen," she heard herself saying, her voice all high and tight now, "just don't talk to me like that! If I say I have to study, I do. So there! And if you want to hang around here pigging out on my grandmother's doughnuts, okay, go right ahead. And if you want to wear someone's bracelet, fine. Go right ahead and do that, too!"

She turned then and began to stumble almost blindly out of the room.

"Katie-doll," she heard her grandmother say as she went by the old black rocker. "Katie-doll," in the saddest voice, not cross at all, just tender and sad. Katie knew that voice from somewhere way back, but she was too angry to hear it, really hear it.

"I'll be in my room," she said. "I'll be in my room if you need me to do anything for you."

The last thing she heard as she went out the door was poor Sam, trying like always. "How about your breakfast, Katie? You may not have to study, but you sure do have to eat."

She thought she heard them laugh, but she couldn't be sure, for she'd closed the door to the family room and run down the short hall to her own room, gone in and closed that door, too, and then flung herself on her bed. And when the tears that came threatened to turn into sobs—noises someone might hear and laugh at—she got up and turned on her little portable radio, always set on KOME so that it came in immediately with music that made her forget her problems.

But now Katie Marshall could not forget at all as she lay there under her patchwork quilt, her face buried in her pillow.

It was four o'clock by the time Katie got up, took off her blue pajamas and got dressed. She turned off the radio and could tell that the house was quiet. Cautiously she went to the living room and looked outside. No one in front, either. She felt exhausted and ashamed. She had to call DeeDee and apologize. It didn't matter if Brian Foster had given her ten bracelets; DeeDee was her best friend.

But first she had to find Gran. Gran liked to eat early. Fine, she was starved herself. She'd fix them a great supper. And she'd call DeeDee right after. She went into the family room bravely, ready to apologize for being a dope and disappearing, hoping somehow she wouldn't have to, that Gran would act, just maybe, as if nothing had happened.

And she did. She was sitting right where Katie had left her, the album open on her lap. "Why, Katie," she said, smiling. "You're all dressed. Wonderful. Here, let me show you this picture of your dad with his first car. It was a little second-hand Chevrolet convertible. He saved for it, bought it himself. My, he thought it was something. 'It's neat, Mom, really neat.' That's what he used to say, and then take off, the ways boys do—then, now. Always, I guess."

Katie was everlastingly grateful. She took the album. Together they looked at more pictures, and it was hard to think that the young man she saw was her dad, but she liked seeing the smiling woman who was his mother. Katie realized that Gran had been pretty, she really had.

"Are there any pictures of Mom?" she asked.

"Indeed there are, and my, she was a good-looking girl, Katie. Is now, too. And you look just like her." Gran patted her cheek. "We're coming to the big romance section in a few pages. I have it all marked off: John and Nancy, college, wedding, graduate school, first baby—well, that's you. First and only . . ."

Then she broke off. "But let's save those for later, Katie. It must be five o'clock by now. You're bound to be good and hungry, dear, and I'd love to fix you some supper."

Katie smiled. She felt better, she really did. Gran made her feel better just by not saying anything about that morning, by not asking any questions. She hugged her grandmother. "No way are you going to fix any old supper," she said. "I'm going to make us some famous California clam chowder. It's got zucchini and carrots in it and onions, of course. I'll bet we can make it right out of your garden in the front yard before the summer's over," she added.

"You think if we dig deep enough we'll find clams?" Gran said.

Together they laughed, and together they went about supper, eating finally on the family room table, just the two of them.

"Fabulous, as your friend DeeDee would say," Gran sighed as they finished. It was good, too. Katie had remembered to float a pat of butter in each bowl and sprinkle on some fresh parsley, and Gran had made some cheese bread. Better even than San Francisco sourdough, Katie thought. And for dessert she had a root beer float.

"Fabulous," she said.

5

It wasn't so hard to make up with DeeDee. They'd had lots of little squabbles growing up together. Sometimes one had to call up, sometimes the other. It was easy to forgive and forget with DeeDee, because they really were true friends, and whoever was wrong was sorry.

So calling was almost just going through the motions.

"Hi," the caller, the culprit, would say. "It's me and I'm sorry I was such a dummy."

"Oh, you," the other would answer. "You nut." Then they would laugh and talk nonstop for the next hour, or hang up and one would run to the other's house, where they would talk for hours more.

It went the same way this Saturday night. Yet

both Katie and DeeDee knew something about it was different. It was hard to say what. Maybe they were just getting older. Maybe they were changing, growing apart. No, that couldn't be, it couldn't. Maybe, Katie thought to herself after the long conversation with DeeDee was over, maybe it's that what we were cross about all those times before just wasn't important. It hadn't mattered, and in fact, by the time they'd hung up the telephone, they couldn't even have said what the fuss was all about.

But this time it did matter. It did to Katie, anyway, and she thought somehow it did to Dee-Dee, too. It mattered because it was about Brian Foster. And just thinking about Brian made her feel funny and happy and scared and weak—and mostly made her want to be with him and worry about whether he wanted to be with her.

Of course, getting those feelings all mixed up with seeing him sitting on the floor beside DeeDee and taking her hand was just plain silly. The bracelet, for heaven's sake, turned out to be a bright red button Brian was carrying around in his pocket that said "Run for Your Life," and he'd fastened it onto some braided rubber bands, also in his pocket—all this while Katie had been out of the room getting Gran's photo album, and as she'd come in, he'd just gone over and presented it to DeeDee.

How could she have acted the way she did!

"What do you think he thought of me, DeeDee?" she mourned to her friend.

"Look, Katie, Brian Foster is just the nicest guy I ever knew. Well, maybe not nicer than Sam. But

yes, maybe he is." She giggled over the telephone.
"I mean, yes, you acted like some tweaked-out
number. But I'll bet he won't even be mad at you.
I'll bet he'll call you tomorrow after church. And
when he does, just say, well . . ." DeeDee wasn't
on too sure a ground when it came to lovers'
quarrels, but she was determined. "Just say the
kind of thing you say to me," she finished. "Tell
him you behaved like a dummy and you're sorry.
It's the truth, after all!"

"DeeDee, you're a genius," Katie said. And
they hung up.

Katie laid back in her bed then and snuggled
down, pulling her patchwork quilt around her. It
had been a long day and a confusing day. Things
had seemed to go first one way and then all of a
sudden another way. No wonder she felt tired. But
she felt good, too, because somehow things had
turned out all right, with Gran, with DeeDee, and
she was sure with Brian, too. DeeDee was certainly right. Brian would call tomorrow. It was such a
wonderful thought. She stretched out under the
covers and turned over, expecting to drop right off
to sleep the way she usually did after a good day.

Instead, though, Katie found herself thinking
about Brian Foster—the fierce look in his blue
eyes, the way a flat, blond curl just hid the top of
each ear, the feel of his hand taking hers, and oh,
more: the feel of the two of them pressed together
for just that moment out there on the front lawn,
she being held there by Brian and not ever wanting
to move. *I am in love,* she thought and slipped off
then into the most delicious daydream about herself and Brian Foster.

She was the queen of the homecoming parade. She rode on a golden throne at the end of an immense float drawn by a long, shiny, white limousine; and there she held sway over a court of kneeling maidens, all members of the senior bunch, subservient now, at her feet on the red velvet floor. She wore a gown of ice blue velvet, and when she raised her arms to the cheering crowds that lined the streets along which she slowly moved, cascades of heavy, white lace fell gracefully from her sleeves.

Slowly she inclined her head, acknowledging the cheers of her subjects, accepting them as only her due, while the float, which had now somehow become a queen's coach and she a real queen, moved toward the town square. Bells rang from the four towers at each corner of the square as the open coach, drawn by six snow-white horses, came into view and her massed subjects pelted her with garlands of blossoms, the sounds of their voices rising as she turned her head to the tall man standing just behind her, taking his hand and gently bringing him closer, closer, until he stood directly at her side.

He was dressed in scarlet doublet and hose and wore a silver jerkin over his silken white tunic. He was her prince; she had chosen him. She had given the sign to her subjects that she was to be his, and he hers. He bent, he pressed his lips to her cheek, he whispered, "Kate, my love, my queen, my darling." He knelt, drawing his sword as he did, offering it to her, and she took the bejeweled hilt, touched him ever so lightly on the shoulder and said, "Arise, Sir Brian." And as the cheers rose to a frenzied pitch, he took his place at her side.

Then, as she turned to him, the scene changed. The scarlet doublet became orange jogging shorts, the silken tunic a sleeveless white track shirt and the sword a drum major's baton, and Brian was leading the Linda Vista marching band. It was running alongside the float playing "Hail to Our Alma Mater," and a chorus sang, changing the words to, "Hail to our lovely queen, hail, hail, hail!" Cameras flashed, and a man yelled, "Get down, girls," to the kneeling court. "We want to get shots of the queen."

Dutifully the senior girls crouched even lower on the floor of the float as the cameras continued to click, and then over their heads came another voice, speaking directly to her. "Miss—the beauty in the blue gown. No, not you," a slick, rich-looking man said to one of the girls who simpered at him. "I want the queen. Her name is Kate Marshall. I want to sign her for my modeling agency. I must have her. I've got a contract right here. There's a *Seventeen* cover she'll be perfect for—perfect!"

He leaped up onto the float and tried to grab Katie's hands as they were stretched out to the crowd, but Brian Foster stepped firmly between them. "Take your hands off the queen, mister," he said. "Back off. Miss Marshall is not signing any contracts right now. There are too many offers to consider. You'll just have to get in touch with me later."

"With you? Listen, I want the queen, Marshall. . . ."

"Miss Marshall to you," Brian said firmly. "And as I said, you'll have to see me. From now on, I'm handling everything for Kate Marshall."

The man faded into the crowd on Linda Vista's main street, the band played louder and dogs everywhere sat up barking. . . .

Dogs barking . . . Drowsily Katie snuggled deeper into her bed and turned over, half awake. What on earth? Beauty. Beauty was barking again, and Bozo from next door—both barking. She must have fallen asleep, must have been dreaming . . . crowds, dogs, a band. Music—she could hear loud music. She stirred, opened her eyes and found she'd left her little portable on. It was sign-off time, and they were playing "The Star-Spangled Banner." Oh, but what had she been dreaming? Of Brian. It had been so wonderful. He was a prince, a champion and her protector. Sleepily she reached out, snapped off the radio and turned over, saying, "No woofing, Beaut. You hear? No woofing."

Then Katie Marshall curled up, murmuring the name *Brian* as she slipped off to sleep, this time for good.

Brian Foster, either as the prince of Katie's dreams or the star of Linda Vista's track team and the light of her fifteen-year-old life, did not call after church or any other time during an interminably long Sunday. Nor did she see him at school, either Monday or Tuesday.

Of course, DeeDee tried to comfort her. "He works, you know," she said, "and he has to run all the time. Or he might be sick—I mean, like have a terrible flu."

"Oh, sure. Or be so hoarse he couldn't call on the phone, I suppose," Katie mocked. And she was miserable, so miserable that Miss Cummings in English let somebody else read Lady Macbeth after Katie lost her place twice, and she didn't get to read the "out, damned spot" scene, which she'd practiced forever by herself in front of a mirror. So miserable that Coach Miles said late Tuesday afternoon, "If you're going to take four minutes to do two laps, Marshall, you might as well not suit up!"

How could it be, then, that on the way home the maroon Mustang slowed to a stop beside DeeDee and Katie, still in shorts doing a slow warm-down run, and Brian Foster, totally cheerful and casual, said, "Where have you two girls been?"

Where had *they* been!

DeeDee asked the question for her as the two of them climbed into his car. "What we want to know is where have you been," she said, adding, on impulse, "if you can remember, Brio."

Brian reached across the two girls and pulled the car door closed, then brought his arm back, took the stick shift, shoved into low, then second, then high, and his hand came down on Katie's for just a moment where it rested on her knees as she sat wedged between the two of them. It seemed to her that her heart stopped.

"Around," Brian said, taking no notice of Dee-Dee's impudent "Brio" and not sounding at all mysterious about where he'd been, either, just easy and matter-of-fact, as if where he'd been just wasn't terribly important.

The way Katie felt being so close to him, it didn't seem terribly important any longer to her, either.

It was where he was now that mattered. She felt dazed, light-headed and heard only vaguely the chatter DeeDee was keeping up with him. She did hear him say he'd had a great time at her house last Saturday, that Beaut was a fine dog and her grandmother a neat lady and he hoped she'd let him know when they had the next groundbreaking.

DeeDee said later that Katie had answered, but she couldn't remember. Evidently she'd said, "You're welcome any time, Brian."

"Boy, that was a super comeback—really sparkling!" DeeDee had laughed at her later. "Don't you know how to flirt?"

"I don't," Katie said. "And you don't, either, DeeDee Ross! What did you want me to say— 'Come over any time, big boy?' Or, 'How about tonight, fella? You really turn me on.'" And they'd begun laughing, trying out one outrageous line after another. Why was it so easy to laugh and make jokes with DeeDee, or even Sam, while with Brian (yes, DeeDee was right) she was just like a wooden stick?

Late that Tuesday afternoon the Mustang pulled to a stop in front of Mel's store, alongside an open Jeep with roll bars, a 1957 Camaro, a small pickup on mud tires and two VW Bugs. "The gang's all here, I see," Brian said. "I'll leave you two. I've got to hit the libe and then get back to the track."

DeeDee was already out of the car. Somehow Katie didn't want to see the gang—or anyone. "I think I'll just go on home," she said. She started to get out, too, but Brian put his hand over hers. "Hey, stay where you are. My coach and four is at your command." She blushed fiercely, knowing that in her dreams there had really been a coach and he had been a prince, she a queen.

He drove through the curving streets of Linda Vista then, taking a very long way around to Ivy Lane, for Katie lived only three blocks from the Stop and Shop, and yet this drive seemed to never end, and she hoped it never would. He kept his hand on hers, holding it to the leather seat between them. Once he came to a stop sign and had to shift. When he took his hand away, she didn't move hers, she simply waited for it to be covered once again. She sighed then; she hoped he didn't hear her, but perhaps he did, for his hand pressed hers even more strongly. She could feel the pulse in his palm and her own hand warm and heavy against the leather.

"Can you shift gears?" he asked suddenly.

"Yes, of course I can," she said. "I learned to drive ages ago. My dad taught me. . . ." Then her voice trailed off. It wasn't that kind of shifting gears he meant—not just learning to drive. He meant—her heart raced thinking of it—did she know how to push the stick from low to second to high as he pushed down the clutch and his free hand still held hers or his arm went around her shoulders. She found herself wanting to take his hand that moment and place it against her cheek. The urge seemed irresistible.

But suddenly Brian accelerated furiously, and when they came to another stop sign, he put his hand firmly on the gearshift and kept it there. Within three minutes they wheeled into her driveway. Neither of them had spoken a word since she had said, "My dad taught me. . . ."

Now Brian opened the door for her quickly, and when she got out, all he said was, "I must go, Kate. I must leave right now." His voice was rough. He didn't touch her.

Mechanically Katie moved up the walk toward her house, past the fresh dirt set out with its little zucchini plants, chive, sage and snapdragons. She heard Brian call, "Hello, Mrs. Marshall," and saw that Gran was on the front porch. She heard the Mustang back out. She didn't turn her head.

She loved him. She loved Brian Foster. And he made her miserable.

6

The rest of the week went by in a grim fashion for Katie Marshall. "If being in love is this awful," she told DeeDee on Friday afternoon, "then I just don't want to have anything to do with it."

"But you haven't got a choice," DeeDee pointed out. "You can't help yourself. That's what's so awful and so terrible and so really fabulous!" She was excited to be enjoying her friend's confidence, for Katie had finally broken down and talked about her feelings for Brian, including the renewed misery she felt as Wednesday, Thursday and now Friday passed without a word from him.

Not that she hadn't seen him—from afar, as they were always putting it in those slushy novels. "She worshiped him from afar, they would say. Well, she wouldn't stoop to that. She wasn't going to

worship Brian Foster! But still, whenever she saw
him down at the end of the corridor, her heart
skipped a beat and for a moment it would be as if
she couldn't breathe. And there were lots of those
moments because Brian seemed to be everywhere
—or else she was everywhere. Who knew?

There he was, out in the grass of the amphitheater Wednesday noon with all the seniors, laughing
and talking. And yes, maybe they were having a
class meeting, but couldn't he even come over and
say hello? And there he was in the town library
Wednesday night. True, he was talking with the
research librarian, not any one of those snooty
seniors like Margo Gilman, but was Katie invisible
where she sat at a study table with DeeDee and
Sam? And if he was going to pedal by her house on
a bicycle at 5:30 Thursday afternoon, did he have
to turn on a burst of speed and streak by with his
head bent like he was in some dumb race or
something? She might have been inside, but
couldn't he have slowed, looked, waved—yes,
stopped? He knew whose house it was!

He probably knew she was watching him this
very Friday afternoon, too, although if he had
waved, it would have been hard to tell just who he
meant to single out, because the bleacher stands
were full of girls watching the track team work out:
running laps, doing low hurdles and high hurdles,
taking high jumps in the pit over on the far side and
pole-vaulting into the big foam rubber landing pit
at the very end of the field. Some of the girls, like
Katie, had arrived in the stands after doing laps
themselves. She had found DeeDee, gratefully

taken a long drink from a Gatorade bottle and then sunk back against the next bench up, hot in her sweat suit but nevertheless feeling good after her workout.

Of course, Brian Foster did not wave. Coach Miles would probably have benched any guy who took to waving at girls during practice. But Brian wouldn't have done it anyhow, Katie knew. When he was on the track, he put everything else from his mind and focused on running. Watching him, Katie could sense this and she admired the athlete he was, forgetting for a moment that she had any other feelings for him. Then he began working out on the low hurdles, and she marveled at the way he moved, at the concentration evident in every bit of his body as he cleared a hurdle and hit the ground in stride, off to the next one. He was exciting, graceful; he was just plain gorgeous to watch.

And that's what someone in front of her was saying. "Gorgeous! Isn't he?"

"Who now, Margo?" Katie saw then that the crowd of girls on the seats just below were all members of the Crumb Bunch: Margo Gilman, Lisa Scott, Pam, Terri, Erin, Sandra. She hadn't even noticed them.

"What do you mean, who?" Margo was saying. "There's only one jock in my life. Brio, that's who." There was excitement in her voice. "Catch the bod as he goes over, Lisa. Wow!"

"Totally terrific!"

"Mega!" The comments flew.

"A real stud!"

"Yeah, buffed." It was Lisa again. "Really

buffed. Look at the muscles in those shoulders. *Mmmmmmm!* Ever get your hands on any of that, Margo?"

There were howls of laughter. DeeDee poked Katie savagely in the ribs as they sat listening. And Katie didn't know if the sharp stab of pain she felt was the real one from DeeDee's elbow or a hurt that came from hearing a bunch of girls talking in loud voices about something that was sacred to her, making something coarse out of the very thoughts she herself had had—being close to Brian, touching him. And now here were these girls shrieking out their stupid remarks. Katie felt angry and in some way deeply wounded. It was not something she could talk to DeeDee about—not DeeDee or anyone.

"I think the matter with you," DeeDee was saying to her that Friday afternoon walking home, "is that you just take things too hard, too seriously, for gosh sakes. You're always finding something wrong or something that hurts or something that makes you suspicious." She nodded sagely. "Yeah, that's it. Lighten up your act. That's what Sam would say."

"Sam," Katie said. "We haven't seen much of him, either."

"Maybe you haven't, but I have!" DeeDee grinned at her.

"DeeDee Ross! When? I mean, how . . ."

"Never mind. When two people care, it can all be managed." She laughed. And Katie did, too. She'd been selfish thinking only of her own grim feelings, and here was DeeDee, her best friend, falling in love, too, and having a wonderful time.

"All I'm saying, Katie, is that what we know about Brian Foster is that he studies like a demon, runs most of his spare time, is out on the track morning and afternoon, heads up the senior class and holds down a job half the weekend."

"Okay, okay. Enough."

"I mean, how could he have time to see much of a girl, even if he wanted to?" DeeDee asked.

"Is that what Sam said?" Katie shot back. Because it sounded like Sam; he was one of Brian's big admirers and defenders, too.

"Why don't we leave Sam out of it?" DeeDee sounded suddenly cross, and Katie was instantly contrite.

"DeeDee, I'm sorry. Honest." The two of them were passing the small park where once they'd played soccer and watched the boys play Little League baseball. There were little boys out there now, fielding balls and batting and hollering. "Hubba, hubba! Way to go! Safe at second, ump, safe!"

The girls stood leaning for a moment against the chain link fence behind home plate. Funny. It hadn't been so many years ago. Life had been so simple—just get on base and head for home.

"I suppose you and Sam have problems, too," Katie ventured.

"Oh, not so many, I guess." But DeeDee sounded serious, and her eyes looked a little worried behind her big glasses. "Maybe the biggest problem is just something so dumb as wishing Sam had a car. I mean, he could use it on his morning routes; it would make a lot of sense. He's so tired by the afternoon he can scarcely get over the low hurdles, much less work on the four-forty sprint Coach wants him to run."

Katie had to laugh. "Tired after a hard day's work, you're saying. You sound like Mom talking about Dad."

DeeDee laughed, too. "You mean like the worried little wife? Not me! I may never get married."

"Bet you will," Katie said.

"Okay, and I don't take your bet," DeeDee said. And together they moved off away from the park and the ballgame, walking more slowly. "I guess the car thing, well, it's more than just the morning paper route."

Katie understood then. "You mean the two of you. You haven't any place to be together."

"Yes," DeeDee said quietly. "Ever been in our house between three in the afternoon and ten at night?" She sighed. "Four of us, not counting Mom and Dad, and at Sam's there are five. The two biggest families in Linda Vista and we had to get together." She shook her head and then added shyly, "Not that we want to really do anything, Katie. You know, like make out."

"Look, I know. You don't have to explain. You just need to be alone, to be close sometimes."

DeeDee nodded, and the two girls walked away in silence. But Katie's thoughts went on. How close? How close did they need to be? Did DeeDee ever have the feelings she had? And was she scared to admit she had, even to herself?

"If we—I mean he, Sam—had a car," DeeDee

said a block later, "we could run in the hills sometimes. I think Mom would let me if I was with Sam."

"That would be really great," Katie said. Instantly she thought of running in the hills with Brian. And if they came to a little valley, by a stream, an old oak, and they stopped running . . .

"Those seniors go out there all the time." It was DeeDee again.

"Who? Oh, them. You mean those glitzy girls."

"The Crumb Bunch. Right. I guess their parents think they're old enough. And a lot of them have cars, so transportation's no problem. I heard that Margo Gilman say she was going out there tomorrow morning. Probably because her dear Brio runs through half of Woodlands Park on Saturdays training for cross-country. Didn't you hear her? They're all going out there."

A wave of powerful emotion swept over Katie. What was it? Anger? No, it was something stronger, or at least different from just anger. It was not a feeling she remembered ever having. Yet even as she told herself that, the name for it came: jealousy. She was jealous. That was it, and she gave in to it, letting herself experience it. In that moment she hated Margo Gilman with real intensity, and she hated the whole Crumb Bunch right along with her. *If I had a car,* she thought, *I'd go out there myself. I would!*

And suddenly she was saying out loud to DeeDee, "I'm going out there!"

"Out where?" DeeDee was staring at her, puzzled, even startled, it seemed, by the passion in her friend's voice.

Then as quickly as it had come, the anger subsided, and Katie regained control of herself. But the plan that had flashed through her mind stayed with her—and the determination to do it, too. When she spoke again, only the tone of her voice had changed. "Listen, DeeDee, I've just come up with the greatest idea since wheels. I mean, really wild. Why don't we go out to the park ourselves?"

"Out to Woodlands?" DeeDee stood stock still on the sidewalk. "Are you crazy or something? We can't go out there. Our parents won't let us."

"Well, who said anything about telling parents?" Katie asked.

"Katie Marshall, you wouldn't do that!" DeeDee said, then added firmly, "but if you would, I wouldn't. No way would I do that."

And they began a familiar battle of words and wills then. How often, when they were younger, had it gone on: Katie making a dare, DeeDee saying, "No, no, never," but finally, always, giving in? Not that they ever did anything very awful, Katie reminded her, and they weren't going to now. "You know you're going to do it, DeeDee Ross. You just are. It isn't anything bad, after all. We're just going to run in the park like half the people in Linda Vista do on Saturday mornings."

"But . . ." DeeDee interjected.

"No buts." DeeDee still looked unconvinced, and Katie gave her the old double whammy then. It had always worked before. "If you don't go," she said, "I'll go by myself. I will, I really will."

It worked, all right. DeeDee, always the loyal friend, had paled at the thought of Katie off on her own doing whatever terrible thing it was—soaping Mr. Beasley's windows on Halloween night; climbing to the top of the steel girders of the three-story office building going up at the new mall, and at nine o'clock at night no less; or throwing water bags through the window of little Billy Ross's secret clubhouse during his tenth birthday party. And boy, that had been the best birthday party he'd ever had! What a glorious fight it had been.

"Remember your brother's birthday party?" Katie said.

"Sure I do," DeeDee said, but she didn't smile. "This is different, though, Katie. It's supposed to be dangerous for girls to run in the park."

"In broad daylight—two of us—on a Saturday morning? The paths are so full of runners that the only danger will be getting separated and lost in the crowd."

"Come on, Katie, be serious."

"I am serious. And tomorrow we're going. Meet you at the corner of Oak and Hawthorn at seven sharp."

"Oh sure," DeeDee said. "Seven sharp. Oak and Hawthorn. Just maybe a good eight miles from the park gates. And just how, Katie Marshall, are we supposed to get there?"

"Easy," Katie said. The truth is she hadn't thought of transportation, but she acted as if she had. "We'll hitch." Now DeeDee looked really shocked. "Come on," Katie said, "get that expression off your face. I didn't say we were going to get in a car with some kook, did I?" DeeDee was shaking her head. "What we'll do is meet at the corner of Oak and Plaza instead. There's a bus stop there. That's it. We'll just sit—no, stand—there by the stop, and when some nice lady pulls up and says, 'Where are you headed for, girls?' well, we'll hop in."

"At seven in the morning this nice lady is driving by?"

"Sure," Katie said. "Maybe she's been to early church, or she has to take her husband to work at the hardware store."

"Oh, sure," DeeDee said. "Anyhow, we are not allowed to hitch rides, Katie Marshall."

"It'll work like a charm," Katie went on as if she hadn't heard a word DeeDee said. "Trust me, DeeDee. Like always. Like the old days."

They were at DeeDee's house now, and Katie kept walking. "Can't we take Beauty?" DeeDee's voice came after her, worried, and Katie smiled. For that question meant DeeDee had given in.

"Of course we can't," she called over her shoulder. "She's too big. Besides, people don't pick up dogs. We'd never get a ride."

"Oh, Katie!" DeeDee's voice was almost a wail.

Katie stopped and turned around. When DeeDee got this nervous, the best thing to do was to act extra calm and hand her some orders. And that's what Katie did now. "Okay," she said, "tomorrow at seven, DeeDee. Corner of Oak and Plaza." She started walking again. "And don't call me up tonight. Because it's all settled."

Katie set her alarm that night for 6:15, and after pulling the alarm button, she put the clock just inside the drawer of her little bedside table. She certainly didn't want anyone else to wake up, even

Beauty, or especially Beauty, who was supposed to sleep on the Indian rug in the family room but tried if she could to ease herself into Katie's room before Katie closed the door at night. Of course, Beauty would beg to come along if she woke up. She always knew when Katie was off for a run. Well, this time she couldn't go. There was no way, as she'd told DeeDee. Katie would have to keep Beaut quiet with a quick bribe, a dog biscuit, the bone-shaped cheese ones she loved, and then a big hug and then get out of the house in a flash, leaving Beauty wagging her tail—she hoped.

She would also leave a note stuck on the refrigerator door with the seashell magnet. She already had it written. It was short, simplicity itself. "Forgot to tell you," it read, "promised DeeDee to run early this A.M., then picnic in the park. See ya, but don't know when! Love, K." Then she had added on impulse, "Don't worry about me!"

Katie thought the note a masterpiece. There was not a lie in it. Sure, the word *park* was a little vague. Or to be honest, misleading. There was no way Mom and Dad would think park meant anything but the little playground five blocks away, although only a dum-dum would ever want to picnic on its pitiful scrubby lawn with three old carved-up picnic tables crowded under one lone oak tree right next to a bunch of noisy little kids playing Saturday morning baseball.

But if the note was misleading, it was still the truth; the words were all true. She was going to run with DeeDee, she was going to picnic in a park and she was going to arrive home sometime like a good girl. With the note on her stand and the clock all primed in her drawer, Katie dropped off to sleep without a qualm. Tomorrow, the big adventure.

Katie's first adventure of the next day, however, took place right at home. She did not, after all, slip out of the house as easily as she had planned with a docile Beauty seeing her off, for Katie's plans had not included Gran. She had not even thought of Gran as she whipped out of bed, crept into the bathroom and back and then put on the running clothes she had all laid out on her desk chair: blue running shorts and a new blue and white mesh top over a sports bra that made her feel good because the stretch material fitted so well it was like not wearing anything. Then her old, baggy warm-up pants with the loose legs, still a nice, bright blue. Then her socks and fine new Easter running shoes. Today they'd get their first real workout, she thought, tying the white laces tight.

Finally she picked up her brand-new jacket from where it was draped over the back of the chair. How she admired it. It was blue, with a white front and blue zipper, its blue logo like a medal on her chest. It was wonderfully silky on the outside, fleecy inside, and it had a hood that she supposed would never hold her mane of hair, although she didn't intend ever to wear it, anyway. She had a braided red headband for that. Still, she liked the idea of the hood. It was really neat. She looked at herself in the mirror and on an impulse opened her top bureau drawer, used some blusher, a little eye shadow—Wild Iris—and the barest bit of the pinkest lipstick. She wondered if DeeDee—or anyone else—would even notice.

But she mustn't stand there admiring herself at 6:30 in the morning. Katie, you dope, get going, she thought. But she was pleased with herself, anyway; she couldn't help it. And it was in this mood that she came into the kitchen and found Gran with Beauty, who had her morning goody already and didn't seem to care much whether Katie was there or not.

Gran was as surprised to see Katie as Katie was to see her. No wonder. She hadn't seen Katie up before ten on a Saturday morning since she'd arrived. "Katie-doll!" she exclaimed. "Good grief!"

"Gran! Hi. Gosh, I didn't think you'd be up," Katie began. But that sounded pretty silly. Wasn't Gran always up every single morning before anyone—and out to greet Sam O'Neill on the front patio? Of course she'd be up on Saturday morning. Well, darn it! Katie would just have to get out all the faster and with no noise and without doing any explaining, either. Because the truth was that Katie was not much good at fibbing, and if she began to tell Gran all about her morning run, the next thing you know she'd be talking about the park—the real park, Woodlands.

Katie saw now that Gran was making a pie. Keeping her voice low, she said, "That looks like rhubarb pie, Gran. Neat." She grabbed a quart of orange juice from the refrigerator. "I'm going running with DeeDee," she said. "I'm not even going to have any breakfast. We'll have a picnic later," she added. "DeeDee's bringing it."

"Why don't you wait twenty minutes, dear? I've got johnnycakes in the oven for the children."

("Can you believe it," Katie had told DeeDee, "she calls my mom and dad the *children!*")

"No, no, Gran," Katie interrupted. "I've got to take off. DeeDee's already waiting."

As she drank her orange juice and stuffed two apples and a jar of Gatorade into her light pack, Katie watched her grandmother working on the pie. She was talking to herself. "I'd rather have made mince—Johnny loves mince—but I couldn't see mincemeat on any of Nancy's shelves. A shame. Maybe I could make some this year. No earthly reason to wait until Christmas. I'll just get some down in a crock right away soon. Oh, my, he does love mince. Still and all, rhubarb's nice this time of year. This'll be dandy." She was chopping rhubarb into short lengths and heaping it into the crust. Katie's mouth watered; she loved rhubarb pie. "This time next year I expect we'll have our own rhubarb," Gran went on, "right in the front yard. Seems to me maybe we ought to put it right next to the fence, alongside the artichokes. It would look pretty there, add a little color. I'll ask Nancy what she thinks. Or Katie . . ."

Then she shook her head, suddenly seeing Katie. She looked surprised. "Well, good grief," she said, laughing a little. "I was way off somewhere, wasn't I?"

Katie rinsed her glass, picked up her pack and started for the living room door. As she went by the refrigerator, she quickly slipped her note under the magnet. "I'm leaving a note for Mom and Dad," she said a little self-consciously. "You have a good day, Gran." (Honest, she sounded like the checkout woman in the supermarket!) "Bye, now."

"You're not taking Beauty?" Gran asked.

"No, not this morning." Katie tried not to sound irritated. She was almost at the door.

"Wait, Katie," Gran said, and Katie had to stop. "I don't remember what time you said you'd be home."

"I didn't say," Katie said, really in a hurry now. "But you know," she made her voice as casual as she could, "like all good girls, home before dark."

"All right, dear, all right," Gran said. "I'll tell them when they wake up, and I'll be sure they get your note." She seemed about to say something more, but Katie had no patience.

"Stay, Beaut, stay!" she commanded the old black dog who wanted to follow her. Darn and double darn! Would she ever get out without everyone in the house waking up?

As she opened the front door at last, she heard Gran call after her, "Now you just have a fine time, Katie-doll. Everything's all right here at home. You just take all the time in the world and have all the fun you can."

If she said any more, Katie didn't hear, for she had closed the door and was running out the drive, heading as fast as she could for the corner that turned toward Oak. Five minutes and she'd make it to Oak and Plaza. It would be seven on the dot. And yes, she was going to take all the time she wanted and have all the fun in the world.

What Gran had wanted to say but had not said Katie did not discover that early spring morning.

7

Wow!" DeeDee, sitting faithfully on the bench at the bus stop, let out an appreciative whoop as Katie ran into view. "You look great," she said, and as Katie came closer, she added, "and you've got some blusher on, too, Katie Marshall. Don't kid me!"

"So?" Katie said casually.

"Not to mention eye shadow." DeeDee giggled then. "As if it won't all roll right down your face after four minutes of running."

"It won't," Katie said. "It's guaranteed to stay on, even in a swimming pool."

"Yeah, I'll just bet," DeeDee said. Then she acknowledged, "Nice with your new jacket, though, I've got to admit. Fab, in fact. How did you ever save enough after putting in for your shoes at Easter?"

"I didn't have to. Gran gave me some money."

"Lucky you."

"In a way, I guess. I almost wish she hadn't, though. She does so many things. I don't know; it makes me feel awful sometimes, DeeDee."

"How come?"

"Because I'm not very nice to her, I guess."

"You can say that again! Sam says . . ."

"Oh, no," Katie said, "not Sam again."

"Again and again," DeeDee said, grinning. "You think he might show up at Woodlands, too?"

"Won't everyone? Maybe we can have a student body assembly."

"You nut, Katie."

They laughed together, and Katie let the marvelous feeling of their morning adventure take over. "On your feet, DeeDee," she said. "Look ready but not too eager. And if some real jerk starts to pull over, sit down on the bench and put your glasses on."

DeeDee had spent some Easter money of her own on contact lenses. She wasn't really used to wearing them and had to switch sometimes during the day, so Katie knew she'd have her big, black-framed glasses with her. "And I'll put this hood up and pull it down over my face." She did this as she spoke, then lifted it suddenly. "Boo!" she said, waving her hands at DeeDee and sticking her tongue out. "That scare you?" And because it was so silly and of course no one in the world would be scared of Katie Marshall acting like such a goofball, they both laughed uproariously.

It was laughing like this that made them completely unaware that a car had stopped. When a voice called out, both girls jumped. But it was a feminine voice, and in a matter of seconds they were in a perfectly respectable car headed for the foothills. It had happened just as Katie had predicted. A nice older woman had asked where they were going, and when they both said, "Woodlands Park," she said, "Hop in. I live on Upper Ridge Road, just a stone's throw from the gates. And isn't it a marvelous morning for a run?" she added as they climbed in.

What a relief it was for each of them, although they never let the other one know. The way this woman acted toward them made what they were doing seem the most everyday thing in the world; it confirmed their status as grownup young women who were just going about the pleasant business of enjoying a Saturday morning. As they wound up into the hills where the houses became sparser but much bigger and set back behind gates and hedges, they both began to feel at ease and then actually cheerful, the way they had wanted to feel all along but hadn't managed to until this minute.

They even exchanged names with their chauffeur. She was Mrs. Rutledge. Fortunately her children were all grown up so that she didn't know their parents, "though I know who Nancy Marshall is, dear," she said to Katie. "I've heard her name at the Art Club."

It all went so well that by the time Mrs. Rutledge let them out at the huge redwood gates to the park, already open for the day, they were in a full holiday mood and ran on inside as if they had not a care in the world. And as they waved their thanks and took off, the truth was that neither of them thought once of the Crumb Bunch, or of Brian, or of Sam or of anything at all but the sheer joy of the sunny morning and the wide, dirt path that carried them off into the hills.

They had passed two older men running and two girls riding horseback when Katie saw that the path branched into three trails ahead of them. "Let's take the upper trail there, DeeDee," she said as they still ran. "We can get in some good hill work."

"Oh, come on, Katie, we're supposed to be having fun. Let's take the lower one. I'm already sweating."

They were approaching the fork. Katie didn't want to break her rhythm, so she simply took off on the middle trail, calling, "Come on, DeeDee, this one doesn't look so bad."

Presently, as she, too, began to sweat a little, Katie broke her stride and came to a stop. "What we've got to do is find a good place to stow our stuff."

"Yeah," DeeDee breathed, glad to pause. "We'll cook if we go on with all this junk."

"We want some place where we can just drop and eat when we get back," Katie said, looking around her quickly. To their right the open area sloped upward and was covered with chaparral— wild lilac, greasewood, some coffeeberry and scrub oak. There were some big live oaks up on the hill, but they were single and open, not too good a place for hiding anything, much less for picnicking. To the left it looked more promising. The ground sloped downward, and Katie could see that beyond the thin chaparral cover there were trees—oak, alder, willow—and she saw a small buckeye bursting with its blossoms, the showy white spikes they always called horsetails.

"Let's head for that buckeye," she said to Dee-Dee, "the one by the big oak. There'll be a stream on below, I'll bet. It probably runs between the two trails."

They went through the brush and into the trees. There, behind a good-sized rock and under some thick manzanita below the buckeye tree, they stashed their rolled-up warm-up suits and DeeDee's small pack. Katie kept hers so they'd have Gatorade for their run.

"You think we'll have any trouble finding this place?" DeeDee asked.

"It ought to be a cinch. Look for a buckeye in bloom on our right coming back and near the end of the trail. If we miss it, we can start over. It's about five minutes in." Then Katie hesitated. "Not that there aren't going to be other buckeyes around. Maybe we'd better put up a marker at that, DeeDee, and be on the safe side."

Katie went back quickly toward the brush near the path and broke off a branch from a deep blue wild lilac. She thrust this into the low manzanita beside the rock and heaped small stones around its base to anchor it. Then she took off her braided red headband and hung it at the top.

"There," she said to DeeDee. "There's no way we won't find this. It's like a little sign: Buried Treasure Lies Here."

"Yeah," DeeDee said, "it looks buried, all right,

like a new grave. Flowers and all. Our fallen comrade . . ."

"Come on, DeeDee, no smart remarks. We've got to get going. We should be back here by eleven o'clock, anyway, and home by one."

Katie surveyed her work as she started back to the path. "It'll be a neat place for lunch," she said, and when they came to the edge of the trail, she noted with satisfaction that you could just see the red headband over the chaparral.

They ran then. It was a slow pace for Katie, but she didn't mind. She was used to running with her friend and rather felt it was her duty to keep watch over DeeDee, anyhow. DeeDee was short, and chubby. She puffed and got hot and red and dripping after the first mile, and this was true no matter how much she ran. Katie kept right along beside her and gave her the talk test now and then, "just to be sure you're still breathing, you lunkhead," she'd say.

But DeeDee was not a sissy, and she always kept going no matter what, so that until DeeDee stopped this Saturday morning hollering for a drink, Katie went floating along with her own thoughts, down through shaded glens and up onto warm hilltops still green from spring rains, and she began to feel the sense of joy that always came to her, even on the familiar runs along the city blocks of Linda Vista. She supposed it was what some called a runner's high, and she knew there were scorners who would tell you it came from taking in a lot of extra oxygen, from being just plain light-headed. Well, maybe so. She never thought you had to give a name to it, anyway. She just welcomed it and ran on, aware of everything around her in a kind of intense, clear way and of herself as part of it all.

"Stop, I said. Stop, Katie!"

It was DeeDee's voice, and Katie pulled up. She'd almost forgotten her big sister role. If DeeDee had disappeared, she might not even have noticed. "Gosh, DeeDee," she said, panting. "I'm sorry. You okay?"

"Of course I'm okay! Can't a guy stop for a drink once in a while? Whew! I should have carried the stuff myself," she said, grabbing the little pack from Katie and taking a long draft from the plastic bottle. "And sit down a minute, will you? We're not trying to break any park records, you know."

Dutifully Katie sat down in the long grass beside DeeDee, trying not to crush the clump of yellow lupine growing there. She hadn't really wanted to stop, and she knew she'd have trouble getting back again to the feeling she'd been reveling in. In some part of her she knew she wished she were running alone, and that made her feel guilty. A group of runners came by and waved.

"No one we know," DeeDee remarked. "Where do you suppose they all are?"

"Who?" Katie asked.

"Who? Boy! If I ever get dragged into your big deals again . . ." She lay back in the grass, disgusted. "'We have to go up to the park,' she says." DeeDee began to imitate Katie. "'I just gotta get up there and see that those horrible old bags don't get their hands on my Brian Foster.'"

Katie began to laugh.

"Oh, sure, Katie Marshall, laugh your head off. Here we are running all over a park that's off-limits for us and hitching to get here, too, all so you can see your precious boyfriend."

"He's not my boyfriend!" Katie put in heatedly.

"And don't you wish he were!" DeeDee flashed back. "But the point is we get up here on our big quest and an hour later you don't even know why we came! You're a complete blank. You don't remember a thing. Zilch. Zilch city."

"Zilch city yourself," Katie responded. But she wasn't a bit cross. After all, DeeDee was right. In the joy of running Katie had completely forgotten the urgent reason for coming in the first place. A family with a picnic basket appeared on the trail.

"Hi," one of the three little kids shouted.

"Good morning," the father called. "Seen any really great places to picnic?"

"It's nice right here," Katie answered. "Actually, I've been running. I think I sort of missed the picnic tables."

"At twenty miles an hour I can understand," the man said, smiling.

Katie smiled back and then saw the mother looking at her anxiously. "You're not alone?" the woman asked, and Katie realized then that DeeDee, lying down, was completely hidden in the tall grass.

"Oh, gosh, no," she said. "My friend's right here." She poked the prone DeeDee, who with a great effort sat up into view. "See?"

The family went on. Katie sighed. "Honest,

DeeDee," she said, "are we ever going to get to the point where older people aren't going to break out in terror over our every move?"

"I doubt it," DeeDee said, resigned. "I mean, I'll probably have three children of my own and my mom will still want to know where I was when she phoned at ten P.M. Yuk!"

The two girls waved at a troop of scouts on bicycles, each in his khaki shorts wearing a white helmet and sporting a tiny orange pennant attached to an aluminum rod above the rear wheel.

"Orange and white," DeeDee commented. "Linda Vista colors. Let's sign them up for the homecoming parade."

"Why not?" Katie said. A scout leader brought up the rear, an exact duplicate of his charges, only bigger. There had been one up front, too. "One thing you can say for Woodlands Park, DeeDee, is that it's safe. I mean, you couldn't be alone if you wanted to."

"Yeah," DeeDee agreed. "When I think how I was all prepared to disappear and leave you and Brian all alone out in some meadow . . ."

"No, a bosky dell," Katie interposed.

"A bosky dell?" DeeDee laughed. "What's that?"

"I'm not sure. Except it's nice. I got it from Miss Cummings's unit on poetry. It's Keats or Shelley or someone dreamy like that."

"Yuk," DeeDee said. "I'm not so great at poetry. Or running, either, Katie," DeeDee suddenly added. "Let's turn around and head back for lunch. I'm bushed, honest. It's pretty obvious there aren't any LV kids around here, anyhow."

"And if there were, we'd never find them,"
Katie said philosophically. "Because the second
thing you can say about Woodlands Park is that it's
big—really big."

"Big and safe. That's our park," DeeDee said,
and with that the two girls stepped out onto the
path and began to run in the direction from which
they'd come.

Within an hour that Saturday morning their big,
safe park turned into a disaster area for Katie
Marshall and DeeDee Ross. First they got lost—
hopelessly, disgracefully lost. Almost right away
they came to a *Y* in their trail. Running in the other
direction, neither of them had noticed that two
trails had joined. Nor had they seen that the trails
were marked. There were two small, carved, redwood signposts, set about knee-high. One said
Windy Hill—7 Miles, and the other, Indian
Camp—5 Miles.

"Great," Katie said. "Which one were we on?
Did you see any signs back in the beginning?"

"No," DeeDee said, shaking her head.

They stood a moment, each trying to reconstruct
the run to this point, to recognize something familiar as they looked off on each trail.

"Lost, girls?" A jogger stopped.

"Not really," Katie said quickly. "We just aren't
sure which trail we came up on."

"Well, don't worry about it if you're just going
back to the gates," the man said. "They both get
there. All these trails do." He smiled. "I like
Windy Hill myself; it always cools me off. But it's
two miles longer, as you can see."

He ran on. Katie sighed. "No use telling him we want the trail that has lots of wild lilac and a buckeye by a big oak and a rock under the buckeye."

"And a big stick in the ground with a red headband on it," DeeDee finished.

Katie smiled. She was determined not to be worried. She knew from experience that DeeDee could get upset in a hurry when things didn't go right. And after all, they weren't in any big trouble. They could try one path, then the other. There was plenty of time. She managed to communicate confidence to DeeDee—more confidence than she felt.

"Let's take Windy Hill, DeeDee," she said. "One thing I'm sure of is that we didn't pass any Indian camps."

"Yeah, sure," DeeDee said doubtfully, "and we didn't pass any windy hills, either. Remember?" Nevertheless she ran along beside Katie, reassured.

It was Katie who called off the Windy Hill run after what she guessed to be about three miles. She was sure they should have come to their hiding place off the trail by then, but as carefully as she searched the area to her right, she saw no red headband marker. She saw five buckeyes in bloom, though, and even went over to investigate one that was close to an oak tree and looked just possibly like theirs. Nothing. They went back and began to run Indian Camp Trail. When they came to another fork labeled Quarry Basin, Katie kept going, hoping DeeDee didn't notice that this made one more place where they might have taken a wrong turn.

But of course, DeeDee noticed. After they'd run no more than three minutes, she said, "Okay, that's it for this one; back to the last fork." Her breathing was labored as she turned around.

"Wait," Katie said, "we haven't gone far enough on Indian Camp."

"Far enough for me," DeeDee said, lurching on. "I just don't recognize this at all."

Where the fork said Quarry Basin she turned off, but she was scarcely running at all now. Katie could tell how tired she was. They'd have to walk for a while. All right, they might as well try Quarry Basin Trail, she told herself, for she hadn't recognized anything on Indian Camp Trail, either. And DeeDee was not only tired, she was worried. Katie knew that and wasn't surprised when she realized that DeeDee, walking silently beside her, was holding in tears. For a while Katie pretended she didn't notice, even when DeeDee stopped her and asked in a pitiful voice, "Isn't there any more Gatorade, Katie?"

"Of course there is, silly," Katie said, "Here, drink it up."

"I'm not going to take the last drop," DeeDee said staunchly.

"Oh, go on," Katie told her, "take it. But just keep moving. I think we're almost to the lilac patch."

At one o'clock DeeDee began to cry. She just sat down at trailside and let out the sobs she'd been keeping in as they hiked farther and farther on Quarry Basin Trail without a single familiar sign. "Oh, Katie," she wailed, "we're lost. We are."

"Don't be an idiot," Katie said, nevertheless putting her arm around her friend. "We aren't lost at all. You heard the man. All these trails go back to the gates."

"I know, but our stuff—our jackets and pants and my pack—oh . . ."

"Now cut it out, DeeDee!" Katie said severely. "I've got a plan. We won't waste any more time looking for the right buckeye. We'll go straight back to the gates as fast as we can get there. You can run a little, I know you can. Then you can sit down and wait while I go get the gear. I'm bound to find it going the same way again. Simple?"

DeeDee looked encouraged. "Okay," she said, still crying some. "But don't let anyone see me like this, Katie." Furiously she began to blink back her tears and wipe her eyes. Then suddenly she let out a wail again. Three people on horseback stopped. Katie shook her head. DeeDee had rubbed a contact lens out of one eye. Well, at least it gave a good excuse for the tears. They all began to look for the lens—the three riders and Katie and DeeDee, as best she could, still sobbing a little and with only one eye she could see out of.

"I remember on TV when a young man playing basketball lost one," a woman said. "They had to look forever, but they found it," she added encouragingly.

"You won't find this one, though," said a little girl cheerfully. She had stopped off from a family of hikers to join the search and now stood poking her pink tennis shoe into the tall weeds.

Oh, neat, Katie thought to herself. Neat kid. If

the darn thing was down in the grass, this little girl would have ground it to bits by now, or buried it. Not that she wasn't right. They'd never find it down in the weeds and dirt and myriads of tiny wild flowers—buttercups, blue-eyed grass, some violet checkerbloom. Katie was so entranced with the flowers, she almost forgot to keep looking. Could she take some home to Gran? . . .

"Katie." It was DeeDee's wail. "It's no use!"

And it wasn't. They had to give up on the contact lens and pretend it didn't matter, although both of them were thinking ahead even more now to their return home. And if they couldn't find their hidden gear? That meant DeeDee's regular glasses were lost! It was all too awful to contemplate.

"Of course, I bought them with my own money," DeeDee said aloud.

Katie understood perfectly what she was talking about. "Sure you did," she said, "and you can save to make it up. It's only one lens, you know." She tried to be comforting. Actually she was beginning to seriously worry herself. It wasn't just finding their stuff, it was having to find a way home, too, and worst of all, having to face Mom and Dad when she got there.

And what time would that be now? No wonder Katie felt relieved when they rounded a bend and came onto a broader path and saw the gates ahead of them. She felt tired, but she didn't want to waste any time. "You go over by the gates and sit there," she said to DeeDee. "And don't you move. And don't speak to anyone, either!"

"Listen, you're not my mother, Katie Marshall!"

DeeDee flared at her. "I can speak to anyone I want to! You just go get everything and get back here. I'll probably have a ride all lined up."

"Okay, okay, don't flip," Katie said. "I'll be right back."

Katie left DeeDee then and quickly found the original three trails they'd come upon some three hours earlier. She looked down at the little signs carefully set at the mouth of each one. Why hadn't she seen them the first time? She had just been in too much of a hurry. There was Quarry Basin. Fine, they'd just come out on that one. It was the lower trail. And there was Windy Hill, the upper trail. Okay, it was just as she had remembered all along: They'd taken the middle fork, Indian Camp Trail. What she hadn't realized is that the other two trails eventually rejoined Indian Camp. Well, it would be easy now. They just hadn't come far enough back on Indian Camp Trail when DeeDee insisted on turning around and trying something else. All Katie had to do was set off and keep her eyes to the left.

She'd said it was five minutes in. Katie checked her watch and then began to run confidently up the middle trail at a fairly slow pace, searching to the side for a buckeye in full bloom with a telltale splash of red sticking up beneath it. At four minutes she slowed to a walk and began to look even harder. She'd seen two buckeyes, but both too soon. Now there were no buckeyes at all—not a white bloom anywhere—for a stretch of at least half a mile. Had she run too fast—or too slow?

She turned around and went over the whole

stretch again. No luck. The red headband must have been knocked off the lilac branch, or the branch itself had toppled. She'd have to go off the trail and tramp around through the low chaparral looking for the tree, the rock, the branch, the headband on the ground. But she couldn't do it now. It was past two o'clock. She'd have to head for the gates. If she stayed out on the trail any longer, DeeDee would worry, or worse, might even try to come after her. That *would* be disaster!

Katie made herself run at a good pace on the way back. She was tired now, but her training, the regular running every single day, stood her in good stead. Head up, she let her legs carry her and let her mind drift off. Just when it was she realized that runners were approaching behind her and gaining fast, she wasn't sure. But there was the slap of their shoes on the hard ground and then the sound of breathing. Even then she wasn't scared. She and DeeDee had been passed several times that day, for they hadn't, after all, been going very fast.

In an unthinking, polite sort of gesture, Katie slowed to let whoever it was pass. But no one appeared. Then suddenly she heard low laughter. Her own breath caught in her throat. She missed a stride but kept going. She could feel them closer, closer. . . . If she could have uttered a sound, she would have screamed with all her might, because now she could feel them, actually *feel* them just behind her.

And at the very moment when Katie thought she would surely sink to the ground, she was enveloped by hard breathing and coarse laughter as two men came up even with her, one on each side, purposely in stride.

"Hi, beautiful," a voice said. "Mind if we join your run?" The shoulder of the man who spoke brushed hers. She didn't look at him, didn't turn her head one way or another. She just kept going, praying desperately that she wouldn't drop. What did they intend to do?

"Anyone ever tell you, you were built for running?" It was the voice on the other side.

Funny, she thought. Someone *had* told her. Coach Miles. And Brian Foster had been standing there. She wished he were now. But the thought of him made her determined to keep running.

"Built for a lot of things, I'd say," the first voice came back. "Not for talking, though, I guess."

"Maybe she's winded."

"Good thinking, Mac. We should all take a break and have a beer." He began to pull up. He took hold of Katie's arm. Desperately she looked for someone. The trail that had seemed so full of friendly people was empty. She must scream, and right now.

But then there was a shout behind her, long and loud. If she had screamed, she'd have been drowned out, she thought later.

"Hey-ey-ey-ey!"

They all stopped, and for Katie the moment of terror was over as suddenly as it had begun. A young woman came running up, red-faced but grinning. She had a beer can in her hand. "Where the heck did you two jerks go?"

"Trail blazing," one of them said, nodding his head toward Katie and winking.

"Sure, we thought we could add to the party," the other said, "but I don't think she's interested." He shrugged.

The young woman surveyed Katie briefly. "Leave her alone, she's only a kid," she said, and then she waved off to someone catching up to them. "Here we are, Midge! Where's Eddie? How do you like these guys," she said as the woman named Midge arrived, "trying to make time with a teenager out running all by herself. I guess boys will be boys." She shook her head. "You better run along now, honey," she said to Katie. "You can see the trails aren't safe around here."

They all laughed hilariously.

Humiliated, raging, Katie took off. All she wanted was to get away, out of there. She'd panicked, and as it turned out, over nothing but a bunch of dumb clucks! And worse, she'd been made a laughingstock. They thought she was just a kid. That's all. Just a dumb kid. Blindly Katie turned on the speed. No matter that her legs began to seem heavy and her breath to sear her throat. To heck with oxygen debt! She had to get to the gates, to DeeDee and home.

Minutes later, though it seemed forever, Katie came flying out on the wide trail that led to the gates. She could see lots of parked cars and people, too, coming and going. She strained to catch sight of DeeDee's short figure. Nowhere. She ran straight up to the gates, frantic, and all but crashed into a group of girls.

"Hold it, Marshall!" someone shouted. "You made it."

"Whew," came a voice she recognized, "at last! We can all go home, both infants accounted for."

It was Margo Gilman who spoke—Margo, decked out in the middle of that warm Saturday afternoon in an orchid-colored velour warm-up suit. But of course, it was obvious she hadn't been running. Not a silky strand of her long hair was out of place, and the eye shadow that matched her suit was as fresh as it had ever been. How Katie herself looked, she couldn't imagine. But there was no place to hide. She was standing there right in the center of the Crumb Bunch in what was surely the P.W. moment of her life.

"I got us a ride." She heard DeeDee's voice and located her at last on the fringe of the group. She didn't look too happy. No wonder.

"That she did." It was Lisa Scott. "It seems you two hitched out here, looking for kicks, I guess, and got lost. Is that the scenario?"

Katie said nothing. DeeDee spoke for them. "That's right. We sort of got lost, like I told you, and Katie went back for our stuff." DeeDee suddenly saw Katie's empty hands. "Hey, gee whiz, Katie, where? . . ."

"Never mind," Katie cut her off. "I just didn't have time to keep looking, that's all." She tried to sound airy about it. "Actually, I ran into some people. . . ." It was true in a way.

"Yeah? Anyone we know?" Lisa asked.

"*Uh-uh.*"

"Look at her blush," Margo said. "Maybe she found Brian Foster after all, out in the south forty. We all know that's what you came for, kiddo."

Katie was furious, but she kept her voice even.

"Listen, Margo, it's neat of you to offer to drive us home. But my parents are due any minute to pick us up." She fixed her eye on DeeDee.

"Oh, sure, I'll bet." Margo looked at her, and for just a moment it seemed to Katie that the look was sympathetic. "You can't fool old hands like us seniors, soph," she said, "so why don't you climb into the jeep here and get yourselves home and face the fatal music."

"Come on, Katie," DeeDee said.

There was nothing else to do. Six of them piled into the open jeep with its roll bar which belonged to Margo's older brother. The rest followed in an oversized old Ford station wagon.

The ride home was grim. DeeDee handed her a folded brochure entitled, "Trail Map—Woodlands Park." She said, "You take it. I can't see to read." Katie didn't even open it up.

"They have those in a wooden box on the gates," Margo commented. "I guess you missed them."

They wound back down the hill through the streets with the big houses, all so excited and grand that very early morning with Mrs. Rutledge, all now like a black road heading into further disaster, known and unknown. Katie thought of DeeDee's contact lens, her backpack, their clothes, her new jacket, the one Gran's present had bought. She thought of the brave little note she'd left under the shell magnet on the refrigerator. It had seemed great. Now Katie knew it meant only trouble. Why had she done it? To see Brian—Brian Foster. They were down onto Plaza Drive now, almost home. Margo was talking to her.

"You know, Marshall, you could have run all

over Woodlands Park looking and you wouldn't
have found Brian Foster. He only runs out there
from six to seven in the morning now. Then he
takes off for Angell Field at Stanford to really
train. It's a new regimen Coach figured out for
him."

So she'd missed him by half an hour at least. She
hadn't even seen his Mustang going down the hill.
What a fool she had been.

"You're a fool to let yourself get some big crush
on Brio," Margo went on. Had she been reading
Katie's mind?

"Yeah, because he's taken," Lisa interrupted.
She was leaning over from the back seat, listening
with relish.

"Don't I hope so," Margo said. "He hasn't
exactly made it all that clear."

"Aw, you know men," one of the girls laughed.
"They're always the last to know their own feelings. Right, gang?"

"Right!" they all shouted.

"So our fearless leader and local sex symbol will
just have to let him know!" shouted Lisa.

"Yay! *Ya-a-ay!*" they all whooped.

"I've got too much competition," Margo said
directly to Katie as the others kept up their chatter
and noise. "And I don't mean you, kiddo." How
Katie hated being called kiddo! "I'm talking about
books and grades and jobs and school applications
and trying to line up the navy, and last but not
least, the enemy of all eager women at Linda Vista,
running. Training. That oval track. That Mr. Miles
—coach of the year—so cute but such a bear for
total dedication. What chance has a girl got?"

"Hold it, Gilman!" a voice called out. "I think this is where she lives."

It was. There was no time at all for Katie to think about what Margo Gilman was trying to say or what she herself would say to her parents. They were wheeling over to the curb in front of 45 Ivy Lane, the station wagon right behind them. She could see the fresh earth that had been the front lawn—and something else, too. Gran, leaning on her cane, halfway down the driveway and coming right toward them.

The day of disaster is in no way over. That's what Katie thought.

8

After all the noise of the girls in the jeep and of the motor itself, it now seemed suddenly silent. Two carloads of girls watched the old woman with her cane coming slowly down the drive at her own uneven pace. Katie saw grimly that she had on one of her funny long dresses that hung crooked to one side, or maybe it was the old lace slip showing.

"Hi, Mrs. Marshall," she heard DeeDee say and felt ashamed that she hadn't spoken first.

"That your mother?" she heard an astonished girl behind her ask, and there were some titters.

Immediately Katie was angry. "Of course it's not my mother!" she said, and as much as she would have liked a moment ago to have disowned any relationship with Gran, she said now, "That's my grandmother. Want to make something of it?" DeeDee told her later that she sounded just like a tough teenage gang member in some movie. Well, she felt like it, too.

"No offense, kiddo," Margo Gilman said. "Does the old gal actually live with you?"

"And what if she does?" Katie answered hotly. "Listen, lots of families live together. It's called having an extended family."

"Extended family?" Margo said. "You mean like extended illness?"

"And you guys just living with your parents," Katie went on, ignoring her, "well, you're just a nuclear family."

"Yeah, we're all bombed!" Lisa Scott said, whooping at her own joke.

Gran had stopped in the driveway now. She peered at them, and Katie realized she didn't see her sitting right there in the front of the jeep. She stood up, started to climb out and heard the dread cry, "Katie-doll! My Katie-did. There you are."

Darn and double darn! Katie thought. *Why, oh why?*

She got out of the jeep, trying to ignore the snickers she heard. "Hi, Gran," she said and kissed her grandmother.

"Best you get along inside, Katie," Gran said, almost whispering. It was a warning, Katie knew. She squeezed her grandmother's arm appreciatively, then turned and said as politely as she could, "Thanks, Margo, for bringing me home." She nodded to DeeDee. "See ya, DeeDee."

"Bet you won't," Lisa said. "You'll be grounded."

"Call me when you get home," Katie kept on. DeeDee didn't say a word. Katie could see she might be about to cry again. "And don't worry about our stuff. I'll drive right back out with Dad this aft and find it. Okay?"

DeeDee just shook her head dumbly, and Katie heard an unmistakable male voice behind her. "You're not driving anywhere at all with me, young lady."

Dad!

Katie Marshall was not a liar. She would like to have thought of an easy way to tell them what she had to tell them, but she would never have made it anything but the truth. Now, with Dad and Gran, she went into the living room where Mom was waiting, and Beauty, too, both solemn, and she told them just what had happened. She took full blame for the whole idea of going to Woodlands Park and of deceiving them by not making it clear what park. "I didn't want to worry you," she said, and that was true as far as it went.

The one event of the day's adventure in Woodlands she did not report was truly for the reason of not worrying the three of them: Katie did not mention her false scare alone on the path nor how frightened it had made her. It wasn't important, anyway, and besides, she was ashamed of her own silliness. She hadn't told DeeDee, and she could see it was best that no one ever know.

"So at least it's a safe place, just crowded with people and perfectly okay for two girls any time."

That is how she finished. No one said anything until Gran ventured, "I suppose it is, John. We can say that. It's plain as the nose on your face."

Dad only said, "Are you quite finished, young lady?"

Katie bit her lip and nodded.

"Because if you are, I think it's my turn to tell my little story of the day." And it was then that Katie found out what her grandmother had wanted to tell her at ten minutes to seven that morning but hadn't. Katie was supposed to have stayed with her grandmother. There had been a reunion of Dad's graduate class at Stanford, just the sixty-five who received masters degrees in engineering that year. They'd talked about it; Katie had evidently forgotten. He and Mom were to have been there at noon. Since she rarely got up before then on Saturdays, of course they had assumed she'd be there when they left. As it was, he had had to go alone; Mom had stayed with Gran.

Now, for the first time that day, Katie felt tears come. "Why didn't you tell me, Gran!" she burst out. "I'd have stayed. You know I would."

"Don't blame your grandmother, Katie Marshall. Shame on you!" It was her mother. "She wanted you to have a good time. That's all. She was thinking of you."

"Which is more than you did for anyone else," her father said.

Katie lowered her head and let the tears fall silently. She saw that Gran was hanging her head, too, as if she'd really done something wrong. She saw how thin her grandmother's neck looked, and she sobbed aloud. "I'm sorry, Gran," she said. "Honest."

As the Crumb Bunch had guessed, Katie was

firmly grounded. One week. No nights at the libe, no trips to Mel's Stop and Shop, no club meetings. Just school and home.

"You don't mean I can't run every day?" Katie asked. She had listened to her sentence in silence, controlling her tears. But not running—the idea seemed impossible. She'd run every single day for a long time now. "I mean, I need to run, Dad," she said, her voice pleading.

"And just why do you need to run, young lady? You aren't in training that I know of. You're not even on a school team. You turned the coach down, remember?"

"But I do need to, that's all. It's like eating," Katie tried to explain. "Besides, running is good for you."

"What's good for you this week," her father said relentlessly, "is to sit right here at home. If you've got to run, try running through your own behavior today—in your head. Maybe you should include the way you've been acting ever since Easter, too. Since your grandmother came, in fact."

That settled that. Katie told herself to be resigned. She had expected punishment and felt she deserved it. Then she thought of DeeDee; she hoped her parents weren't being too hard on her. She should phone. "I'd better go call DeeDee," she said, "so she'll know I'm not going back for our stuff."

"Stay where you are," her father said. "Part of grounding is no telephone calls."

Katie gritted her teeth. "Somebody else better call her, then. She needs to know. Maybe *her* dad will go out there with her!" she said pointedly.

"I can phone," Katie's mother said.

"No need," Dad stopped her. "I'm going out there myself. From what Katie's said, I really don't think it's going to be all that hard to find the lost cargo."

Clearly Mom thought this was a waste of time, but Dad took the park map and made Katie tell him all she could about their hiding place. Describing it made it vivid all over again, so that by the time she finished, Katie was sure her father could find it. She'd find it herself in a flash if she could get back there.

But her hopes turned out to be wishful thinking. Mom was right. Her father came back at around seven. It was still light outside. He shook his head. "Nothing," he said. "I went off the Indian Camp Trail on the left and tramped it thoroughly for at least three quarters of a mile."

"Maybe if you'd had Beauty with you," Gran ventured.

"That's right," Mom said. "She might have picked up Katie's scent on the clothes."

Dad shook his head. "My guess is your gear was stolen, Katie. We can call the park office and make a report. But you did leave a red flag, you know."

"Oh, dear," Mom said. "Your nice new jacket, Katie. And DeeDee's glasses. Goodness, her parents must be upset."

"It would be nice if I could call and let her know, at least," Katie said, feeling bitter. It seemed to her that her parents were unnecessarily rubbing it all in. There hadn't been a cheerful word spoken since she'd walked in the door. Even Beauty hung back close to·Gran. Was it going to be like this all week?

She might as well just go to bed. They'd waited supper for Dad. Well, she didn't want any supper. She said so, and when her father objected, she went right ahead and was rude.

"I'm grounded, remember?" she said. "There's nowhere else I can go. So I guess I can at least stay in my own room if I want to!"

As she went through the living room into the kitchen she could hear her grandmother say, "Now, John . . ."

And her mother chimed in, sounding exactly the same. "Now, John," she said, "she's just mad at herself. That's all. Don't forget, Katie's got some of your temper."

Alone in her room, Katie took refuge on her bed, burying herself in her patchwork quilt. She'd denied wanting supper just to be perverse and to make them feel sorry for her, too. But now she found that she really wasn't hungry, although she hadn't had any lunch, either. Well, she thought, so now I know that disaster takes away your appetite. Because this had certainly been about the most disastrous day of her life. A real P.W. Even using the initials that were her private joke with DeeDee and always made them laugh didn't make Katie feel any better this Saturday night.

Personal Worst is right! she thought. I've just blown about everything I ever even cared about. I lost my new jacket, and that must make Gran feel bad, because it was her money that bought it. And I wasn't very nice to Gran today, either. I left her when I was needed. Oh sure, I stuck up for her in front of the Bunch. But inside I still felt ashamed of

her, even though I know I like being with her when
we're by ourselves.

Then there's DeeDee, my best friend. DeeDee
lost a contact lens and her glasses, besides. And
I'm the one who got her into all this trouble. Just
because I wanted to see Brian Foster, who wasn't
even there, and if he were, he probably wouldn't
have looked at me if I'd run right into him. That
Margo Gilman has decided he's her property; she
said so. How could I ever compete with her? She
knows everything, just how to act with boys and
what to say and how to dress. And she has her
brother's car, too.

Not that a car would matter to me! I could have
ten cars lined up and I wouldn't be able to use
them. Just a kid. A little girl. And grounded!
Grounded for a week. That's forever—a lifetime.
And no running. That's *really* unfair! If I were on
the cross-country track team, well, then it would be
perfectly okay with Dad for me to run any old time
I want to, grounded or not. He's just like the
coach—trying to get me to join the team. Everyone
wants me to do something! No one will leave me
alone. Next thing you know Dad'll start asking why
I even belong to the Joggers Club if I'm not out for
track. . . .

And then it hit Katie. Dad had said no school
clubs. And the Joggers Club was meeting to plan
the float for homecoming this very week. And at
her house! She'd forgotten all about it. Everyone
at school would know now and have a good laugh.
Maybe the club would meet at Margo's instead.
Maybe they'd have a new election and Margo
would be president! It was all too much, the whole

day, all the awful things she'd done. And now this. She began to cry.

Huddled under her quilt, crying, Katie did not hear the door open and close quietly. It was her mother, bringing both the drumsticks saved from supper and a pint of milk. Gratefully Katie ate, and as she wiped away her tears, she told Mom about the meeting and begged for help.

"Don't worry, Katie, I'm sure it will be all right. Dad's not such a bear. After all, what happened today was pretty grim, you know that. We counted on you to help with Gran, and you weren't there. And for the first time that I can remember, you broke a rule we set up for your own protection and fibbed about it, too."

"But it's over and done with now," Mom said, smoothing back Katie's hair. "It won't happen again, I know that. And if you're grounded for a week, the time will fly, you wait and see. Especially with the Joggers Club coming here Thursday," she ended up, smiling.

"You really think it'll be okay?"

"I know it will. After all, as you said, this is where you're grounded. And it certainly wouldn't do for a president not to preside over a very important meeting of her club in her own house. Would it?"

She kissed Katie and left the room.

Quickly Katie got her clothes off and crawled into bed. She felt lots better, and she was suddenly as tired as she'd ever been, exhausted and totally ready for sleep.

But there were two more visitors yet to come. Almost asleep, Katie heard the door open, and before she could turn over, she felt a wet tongue on her cheek. "Beaut," she said and put her arms around the dog.

"I don't see why Beauty shouldn't just sleep right in here tonight, do you?" It was Gran standing beside her bed. She had cookies, of course. She doled them out impartially to Katie and to Beauty and then sat down on the edge of the bed. "Ah, Katie-doll," she said. "Gran is so sorry."

Katie thought she might start to cry again. She was getting as bad as DeeDee. "Gran," she said, "don't say that. Please don't. It was all my fault. You know that."

"Oh, I know. But some my fault, too. I should have kept you from going off. But you see, I thought they'd let me stay alone for one day. And you looked so pretty, so fresh, so happy in the beautiful early morning. I wanted so for you to have fun, to have a good time." She broke off and looked for a long moment at Katie. "And did you have fun?"

"Not really, Gran." Katie sighed. It was true. The trip to the park had been a great idea, but it hadn't worked from the very beginning for the simple reason that she, Katie Marshall, had been doing the wrong thing. She knew Gran understood this; she didn't have to say it aloud. She reached up and hugged the old woman, and Beauty kissed them both.

"You put your pretty head down now and sleep," Gran said, and then as she left, "and don't worry about the giant chocolate chip cookies for Thursday. I'm planning on tripling my recipe."

Katie went to sleep that night with her thoughts

in a jumble. Part of her felt grim and angry. Part of her felt contrite and really sorry for the trouble she'd caused and the failure of the whole scheme: She hadn't even seen Brian and she probably never would. And perhaps, worst of all, she wasn't to be allowed to run. Yet another part of her was saying, "Hey, it's not so bad. Like Mom said, the week will pass. You're president of the Joggers Club, and you get to have the meeting after all. Your mom loves you; your grandmother, too. And admit it, so does your dad."

Not Brian, of course. He didn't love her. But how could she ever have thought he would? Maybe if she fell asleep, right now, she'd dream again of herself as a queen and Brian Foster her prince. It shouldn't be so hard.

It wasn't.

9

Some nice person—she assumed her mother—allowed Katie to sleep late that Sunday morning and even let Beauty out of the room. She awoke to the smell of after-church pancakes and the sound of the phone ringing. She grinned to herself. She was rested, and she felt good all over. She couldn't help it. Let the old phone ring. She didn't have to leap up and answer it. She was grounded. No calls for her. She yawned, stretched, got out of bed pulling on her pink summer seersucker shorty robe and then opened her door, calling out, "Here, Beaut!" the way she did every morning.

But right away Katie realized there was something different about this morning. If the telephone call hadn't been for her, it was evidently about her. She could hear her father in the family room saying, "I never thought of Katie in just that way,

Coach. I don't know. It may be I'm inclined to agree with you."

Coach! Katie stood at the door of the room, transfixed. What coach? Her father waved, his gesture saying at once, "Hi" and "Pipe down." He nodded and went on speaking into the telephone. "But you can understand my position on this whole grounding thing. . . ." Then he listened a bit, then went on, "I hear you, I really do. And you say this young person is thoroughly reliable? Because we just do not let Katie run alone, even right here in our own neighborhood. *Ummm,* I see. All right, then, it's decided." He was nodding vigorously now. "Go ahead and send your stand-in over. You've sold me."

"Dad! What was all that about?" Katie demanded. "Send who over?"

Her father was looking at her in a puzzled sort of way. "Coach Miles says you have great potential as a runner, Katie. He's worried about you not running, even for a week. He seems to think he's got you lined up for the team next year. If it's true, you haven't told me," he said gruffly.

"But who's coming over?" Katie interrupted.

"He says he's got a good, solid training schedule mapped out for you that goes through summer and into next fall. True?"

"I guess so," Katie said impatiently. "I haven't quite decided about the team yet. But the schedule is neat, just what I like to do, anyway—a lot of running every day. Building endurance. That's what comes first."

"Just what he said."

"But Dad, what has that got to do . . ."

"Oh, yes, sure. Who's coming over. Well, I told him your running partner was grounded, too, and we didn't let you run alone. You heard that."

"So?" Katie said. Was she supposed to have some assigned keeper, some glitzy senior girl from the team she didn't even know, go traipsing around Linda Vista with her?

"Mr. Miles must think you're some world-class up-and-comer, Katie," her father was saying, "because he's gotten his top runner to volunteer to jog with you every afternoon this week, beginning today. And you sure were right about one thing. This coach doesn't want anyone to miss a day running. Parents or no. Nice of him, though, to go to so much trouble."

"Who is it, Dad?" Katie was beside herself. "Who's coming over here?"

"Oh, yes. I keep forgetting. It's that young fellow whose name we see in the sports page of the local paper every week." Katie almost collapsed. "Coach says you two know each other—Brian Foster."

"He was here a Saturday or so ago helping me in the garden," Gran volunteered when Katie seemed speechless. "A nice young man, John. You're bound to like him."

Now it was Mom's turn. "You remember where the Fosters live, dear," she said. "Over on Arlington Circle."

"You mean this is Hugh Foster's son? Sure thing. Why didn't I think of that?"

"Better get your clothes on," Mom said. Her

grandmother winked. And Katie fled to her bedroom.

She hurried to pull on her clean yellow running
shorts and the matching tank top with its wide,
two-tone blue stripe around the waist and to get
into her shoes. She didn't forget to pick up her
dirty clothes and stow them in her laundry bag, and
she didn't leave her bed unmade, either. She
attacked her thick hair as ferociously as she could,
wishing her headband were not lost somewhere in
Woodlands Park. She grabbed a blue bow instead
and tied her hair back at her neck. It was the
ribbon she'd had on the day Brian Foster first spoke
to her. It was not something she would forget.

Her heart began to pound. She'd hurried. She
was ready, and now she heard a car pull up in front.
Was she really so eager to go out there? If anyone
had told her yesterday that today she might be
running with Brian Foster at her side, she'd have
thought that person crazy, but she'd have died of
happiness nonetheless. Yet here she was hanging
back. . . .

"Katie!" It was Mom's voice calling down the
hall. "Brian Foster's here, dear, to take you running."

And then she was walking out through the family
room, the kitchen and into the living room. "Hi,"
Brian said. His eyes looked directly into hers, and
he smiled; and suddenly nothing was difficult or
scary anymore. Brian Foster had come for her, and
he stood before her now, tall and handsome. He
wore white running shorts and a white mesh tank
top and an old Linda Vista High sweat shirt tied

loosely around his shoulders; his shoes matched her own.

Katie drank the tall glass of orange juice her mother handed her, nodding when Mom said, "Breakfast later, you two. Or lunch for you, I'd guess, Brian."

"I'd like that, Mrs. Marshall," Brian said. Then he laid his sweat shirt across the back of a chair and turned to Katie, and in a voice that was gentle but still somehow commanding, he said simply, "Let's go, Kate," and she found herself responding. She was out the door and onto the walk as Brian shook hands with her father, saying, "I'll have her back in an hour, sir."

And then he was there beside her, and she was Kate again.

Running with Brian Foster that day and the days that followed turned out to be the happiest experience of Katie's life. At least that's how it seemed to her. Not that their runs were romantic occasions. They weren't. You could sweat just as much running with a boy as with your best friend, she found. But she found that you could laugh just as much, too, and you could feel like a friend. Except for a brief glimmer of this kind of relationship that she had had once in a while when she was with Sam O'Neill, Katie had never felt this way with a boy, not since she'd been in high school, anyway.

It had come about so naturally that Sunday in the late morning as they started off at a warm-up pace along the bike lanes of Linda Vista. She'd found herself laughing, and Brian understood why. "It was like we were going out to the senior prom, wasn't it?" he said.

"Shaking Dad's hand, promising to get me back. In the middle of the morning. It was funny, all right."

He laughed easily and then moved out just ahead of her. "I can't get you back if we don't go anywhere," he called, and she stepped up her pace to come alongside, and they began to run steadily then, not talking anymore.

Katie discovered in those days that running with Brian Foster was different from running with anyone else. She'd always run with someone because that was a family rule. But she'd always made the time her own; she had gone inside herself to experience the joy of running, losing all consciousness of the person beside her other than to pace herself to whoever it was in a kind of automatic way. But with Brian Foster, Katie never forgot for a moment that he was there beside her, that they were running together. There seemed to be a natural rhythm common to them both. She felt it in the way they instinctively matched pace, their feet coming to the pavement in the same instant as if to a beat. She felt it in the flow of their arms and shoulders, close, in unison, moving ahead together. She was conscious even of their breathing—not of his breathing or of hers, but of theirs together. There was a oneness about them as they ran, and the elation of running, the joy of it, was shared. For the first time in her life an emotion was totally, naturally shared. He seemed a part of her. She could not have assigned a name to what he was—

friend, companion, boyfriend. He was not really any one of those, or he was all of those and something more in the sweet, short hours they ran together.

Katie never kept track of the miles they ran nor of the time it took to run them. She'd always resisted timing herself and often didn't wear a watch at all, much less one with a second hand. But she soon realized that Brian did keep track of their runs, and she sensed that when he checked his watch it was not just to be sure he had Katie back home in time. For one thing, Brian's leather watch strap held a chronograph, not a simple wristwatch. It had three dials and various little buttons to push, and she knew he could check for all sorts of things if he cared to—time, distance, intervals short or long. She even became aware that he was timing her and that he was gradually stepping up their pace. She found she didn't mind.

Once he said to her, "Let me know if you feel you're pushing yourself, Kate. I don't want you to do that. Coach doesn't, either."

"I'm fine," she'd answered. "It feels great."

That was Tuesday afternoon, and shortly after this exchange he ran her over onto the grass of the little neighborhood park near her home, slowing down as he did so. "Let's take time out," he said, dropping to the ground. "No one will ever know."

She sat down, too, then quickly stretched out, not in the least self-conscious. "Boy! This feels good."

"It's part of my plan," he said. "We should still get in seven or eight miles in an hour. Okay?"

"*Mmmm,*" she said. She had her eyes closed but was attentive.

"So if I work you up from an eight-minute mile to a seven-minute mile even, then we have ten minutes to talk." He paused and then added softly, "And I like talking with you, Kate."

He didn't touch her, though; he hadn't once on those afternoon runs during the early part of the week, except when he took her hand at the very beginning, urging her out the door, eager to begin their run. Instead, they talked, really talked. She found that even an eighteen-year-old senior, admitted to four universities and something of an idol in his high school, could feel uncertain about his future. That Brian Foster actually worried about what he wanted to do, where he wanted to go, what kind of person he might become, was a revelation to Katie Marshall. But once she understood, she found it wonderful to tell Brian just how she felt about so many things: her future, Gran, her dad, running, even about getting lost on the trails of Woodlands Park. The lost gear had not been turned in or found, though DeeDee's father and Sam had gone out twice to look. And she was to blame.

Brian said he'd talk to her father about taking her out to Woodlands at the end of the week. He had a meet on Saturday, but they could go Sunday, and he was sure they'd find her jacket and DeeDee's glasses safe in the very place she'd left them. He made it sound so simple. Katie felt only a twinge of disloyalty to be sharing with another person the kinds of thoughts and feelings only her good friend DeeDee had been aware of before.

"Are you sometimes even sort of afraid of growing up?" she asked him Wednesday afternoon during their time-out minutes at the park.

Brian laughed. "Listen," he said, "I'm supposed to be grown up right now! That's what my father thinks, anyway. But sure," he added seriously, "sure I feel scared sometimes, Kate. A guy is supposed to know by the time he's six years old that he wants to be a doctor, an engineer or something like that. Hey, I'm still not sure."

"Is that why you might join the navy?" she asked.

He looked at her, surprised. "Where did you hear that, for Pete's sake?"

"From Margo Gilman," Katie answered truthfully and then felt embarrassed. Would he think she sat around talking about him with a group like the Crumb Bunch?

But Brian didn't seem concerned. "Margo. Sure. I should have thought of that. Margo's all right, Kate," he said as if he knew exactly how she viewed that particular senior siren. "She just comes on a little strong."

"She calls you Brio."

"I guess she does," Brian laughed, "but I'll live."

Katie decided she'd file Brian's judgment on Margo for future thought. Maybe "coming on strong" was just Margo's way of hiding feelings they all had. She felt almost wise for a moment, and then the next moment was absorbed all over again in Brian Foster.

"If you joined the navy, Brian, when would it

be? I mean, would you just suddenly be gone forever?"

"That's right," he teased. "I'll board a ship—a flagship, a Nimitz-class carrier—and disappear over the horizon."

"Something big enough so that you can run ten miles every morning before you report to the captain," she responded in the same spirit.

"Right. I'll come ashore once a year in April and run the Boston Marathon."

"I guess I was serious about my question, though," she said.

"The navy, you mean. No, I'm not going to run away and join the navy to see the world. My plan is NROTC at college. I'll be a reserve officer when I graduate. My dad was in the navy during the Vietnam War. This flight watch was his. He was a pilot, you know." He paused. "Or no, why would you know?"

They were sitting on the grass cross-legged facing each other and talking earnestly. They didn't even hear the Little League game just a few yards away from them, so intent were they on each other. "There's just so much you don't know that I want to tell you, Kate. And so much for us to do. This summer, whenever I've got time, we're got to run together—hill running in Woodlands, intervals, maybe pace work by the end of the summer. You should enter a Bonne Belle race next year, Kate, maybe even the Avon Marathon."

It was warm, and Brian peeled off his tank top as he talked. Perhaps it was then that Katie felt a change in the mood between them that afternoon. Involuntarily her eyes dropped from his face to his chest, and just seeing the sun glint on the blond curls there sent an electric current through her.

"Too bad girls can't strip the way guys can, Kate," he said, "because it sure feels good."

As to what might feel good, it was the dizzying thought of placing her head against Brian Foster's chest that came over her, and the impulse to do it was so strong that she simply laid back on the grass and closed her eyes. It was then that he must have sensed that her mood was not the same as when she had lain there relaxed on another day. Now he took her hand and came down on the grass beside her and said, "Kate!" Just that, urgently, close to her ear.

"Way to go! Way to go!" Shouts from the nearby Little League game broke over them, and they sat up instantly, almost guiltily. The same shouts and voices had been there all along, but now it seemed to Katie and Brian as if the words were aimed directly at them. Katie knew she was blushing, and Brian carefully kept from looking over at the baseball field.

"It's time, Kate," he said. He took her hand again but only in a firm, directive kind of way as he pulled her up, grabbed his shirt off the ground and began to trot toward Ivy Lane.

Katie came after him but did not hurry this time to catch up, to come into an even stride with him. Everything was different. She felt hurt but was not sure why. Of course, he was right to start home. They couldn't lie side by side holding hands in the Linda Vista neighborhood park with two teams of Little Leaguers and who knows what other passers-by staring at them. And yes, it *was* time to go home if they were to appear at the close of the magic hour. Still, did he have to be so abrupt? Did he have to take off without her?

In a somewhat ragtag fashion they arrived at 45 Ivy Lane just in time to say goodbye to Katie's parents, who were headed for their monthly bridge club supper.

"Like clockwork," her dad said with satisfaction. "I knew we could count on you being here, Brian. I didn't even hesitate to walk out the door," and he shook Brian Foster's hand, something he seemed to be doing all the time, Katie thought, suddenly feeling perverse. She wished they were still in the park.

"Gran's already starting on the cookies for your club meeting tomorrow, Katie," her mother was saying, "and I've got tacos in there all ready to assemble for your dinner. You must surely stay, Brian."

Even as Brian shook his head, her parents were in the little station wagon and backing out of the drive. "I've got to go, Kate," Brian said.

He hadn't looked at her since they left the park, and he didn't now. He surely would have run off down the block if Katie's grandmother had not appeared in the doorway waving her cane in a friendly fashion.

"The first batch is out," she called. "You two come right on in here and try one."

Brian Foster was too polite to do anything but go inside, eat two giant chocolate chip cookies, declaring them the best ever, and then stay for four tacos. "The good news, Mrs. Marshall," he said after number three, "is that Coach Miles says tacos are not junk food."

"You're right, young man," Gran said, "as long as there's plenty of meat and you put plenty of cheese on top." She pushed the big bowl of freshly grated cheddar across the table toward Brian.

That's the way the conversation took place among the three of them during dinner. Gran did most of the talking; and when Brian talked, he talked to her. And when Katie talked, she talked to her grandmother, too. If Gran noticed any strain, she didn't let on, and Katie was grateful. As Gran chattered on cheerfully, it suddenly occurred to Katie that her grandmother seemed to be feeling a lot better. She must have gained a little weight; certainly her dresses fitted better. Perhaps she was beginning to get over her grief.

"Mrs. Marshall," Brian was saying, "let me help Kate with the dishes. Then I've got to get going. I've got studying up to here."

"I could do them, Brian," Gran said. "I'd be glad to. You two just relax in the other room."

"Don't be silly, Gran," Katie said, feeling embarrassed. "I'm going to do the dishes all by myself. You can go home and study," Katie said then to Brian, and it was the first remark she had made directly to him that evening.

"It's certainly nice that we're all so eager to do dishes," Gran said. "Maybe I'll go watch the news, after all. You two can stay here and squabble about who washes and who wipes." She left for the family room, calling, "And don't you dare let the cookies in the oven burn, either one of you!"

*   *   *

They were alone then. Looking almost grim, Brian handed Katie a towel. "I'll wash," he said. "I'm an ace at it." He turned on the hot water, letting it flow into the plastic dishpan. Silently Katie handed him a bottle of liquid soap.

"She left us alone on purpose, you know," Brian said.

"Yes," Katie answered. He reached across her to put a glass in the dish drainer, but she took it directly from him. Their hands touched; the glass slipped. Their hands clasped, the towel dropped and then they were in each other's arms.

There in the kitchen they stood, locked together. He spoke her name over and over: Kate, that name that was the other wonderful part of her. And then he tipped her head back and kissed her. The anchorman on the seven o'clock news blathered on at high volume, and whether this was because of Gran's slight deafness or because of her tact, Brian and Katie did not know or care as they clung together and Katie let his kiss flow through her entire body. She would never have ended that moment, ever.

But Brian did, thrusting her away—once again rough, almost angry. "Don't you see, Kate?"

Still breathless, she shook her head. Aching to be close to him again, she took his hand.

"No!" he said sharply. "You mustn't." He put her hand away from him. He picked up the towel from the floor, and he straightened the glass in the drainer. "You'll have to do the dishes after all," he said. "I must go."

He left, and the dishes remained unwashed as Katie stood in the middle of the kitchen, miserably unhappy. And presently the cookies began to burn.

Too late, Katie rushed to the oven, and as she took them out, she heard Gran behind her. "I never should have trusted you two," she said cheerfully, and then, "Oh dear, Katie-doll! Where did that boy go?"

"Home," Katie said dully. "He went home."

"Now, Katie Marshall, never you mind." Gran put her cane on the table and began doing the dishes. Meekly Katie wiped. "There," Gran said as they finished, "now I'll just get busy and mix up another batch of cookies. You sit down there on the stool and talk to me."

And Katie did. She just let it pour out and let the understanding nods and clucks of her grandmother wash over her like a healing balm. Within an hour Katie went from feeling that she wanted to die and would never stop wanting to, to finding herself soothed and comforted and possibly ready to face life again. At least she was able to get the cookies out without burning them this time around and able, just maybe, to agree with Gran that Brian Foster wasn't, after all, treating her like a little girl with a crush.

"He's a man, Katie," she said, "and he doesn't dare trust his feelings. You'll come to understand that."

"I won't," she said. "I trust his feelings. And mine, too."

Gran sighed. "You said he was thinking about going into the navy," she said. "Funny, it reminds me of a time at Pearl Harbor years and years ago. But I remember as if it were yesterday. I was out in the kitchen, too, baking something, not cookies, I can't say what. My sweetheart came in calling my name. 'Nora,' he said. His name was David. He was a lieutenant-commander. Ah, Katie, I hadn't seen him for six months. I wasn't even sure he was alive; his carrier had been sunk under him. . . ."

Quietly Katie listened.

"And when I turned and saw him, I could have melted to the floor where I stood. I loved him so, Katie." She spoke Katie's name, but she wasn't really aware of her granddaughter at all. "He kissed me, and I thought the world had stopped in its tracks."

The old woman fell silent, and the room was quiet for a long moment. Then she came back to the present, saw Katie and smiled. "So you see, Katie-doll, that's what it's all about. Love. You're in love for the first time, Katie. No wonder your eyes are so lovely—and so full of misery, too."

Katie looked at her grandmother wonderingly. She seemed a different person, not someone's grandmother at all, and there was so much she didn't know about her. "You said his name was David—your sweetheart, I mean." What a funny, old-fashioned word, she thought. "So it wasn't grandfather."

"Good grief, no!" Gran laughed. "Just an old beau." And there was an even more old-fashioned word. A beau! "It was wartime, you know," Gran went on.

"Is that why you were at Pearl Harbor?" Katie asked.

"Of course. I was there for a year at the naval air base on Ford Island."

"But how could you be at a naval air base?" Katie interrupted.

"I was stationed there, for heaven's sakes," Gran said. "I was at Com 12 Headquarters in San Francisco when they decided women could go overseas, and I was in the first batch out, believe me. We sailed in an old Hawaiian cruise liner. They'd turned it into a troop ship."

It dawned on Katie at last. "Gran, are you saying you were in the navy?"

"Why, of course I was. How on earth else would I be out on a naval air base in the middle of a war?"

"But that's just what I asked you," Katie said, and suddenly they were both laughing together. "You were in World War II, then," Katie said.

"Well, it certainly wasn't World War I," Gran said. "I'm not that old!"

"You were a WAVE, weren't you? A WAVE officer. Why didn't you ever tell me?" Katie asked.

"I don't know, Katie. I guess there just wasn't any reason to. It was so long ago. And to tell the truth, I think your father never did quite approve of having an ex-navy lieutenant for a mother."

"A lieutenant! Is that three stripes?" Katie asked.

"Only two." Gran smiled. Then, seeing the look on Katie's face, she asked almost shyly, "Would you like to hear about it?"

"Would I ever!"

"Come along, then. That album we had out is still in the family room, and it has some pictures, I'm sure." Gran took her cane and motioned for Katie. "I think there's even one of me saluting an admiral on the 'Big E.'"

'*The Big E,*' Katie thought. What was that? Well, she'd find out. Her grandmother had been an officer in the United States Navy. That was a fact, and it was plain fabulous, as DeeDee would say. Wait until she told DeeDee tomorrow—and everyone at the Joggers Club. And Brian. She'd see him then. She'd just ignore tonight, and Gran could tell him all kinds of things about the navy.

10

Brian Foster had not shown up by the time the Joggers Club meeting began at 45 Ivy Lane the next afternoon. But this didn't bother its president too much. Katie knew Brian's training schedule had suffered because of the time he'd spent running with her. She assumed he was making up for some of it today and might even arrive before the meeting was over.

Katie and her mother had opened up the family room so that it was part of the living room, and Dad had brought in the long picnic table from the back patio and put it at the far end. They'd covered it with crepe paper in Linda Vista colors, orange and white, and Gran had loaded it down with platters of giant cookies. The pitchers of fresh lemonade were ready in the refrigerator with lots of ice in the freezer chest. And Beauty was safely shut out in the backyard, her flapping dog door into the kitchen closed tight. Everything was ready.

Just before the first person arrived, Katie's mom said, "I'm going to be back in the sewing room, dear. You let me know if you need me for anything."

"And I think I'll just take this time to catch up on my letters," Gran put in right away.

"You two don't have to disappear," Katie said. "Besides, Gran, I told everyone about my grandmother who was a lieutenant in the navy. They all want to meet you. Honest!"

"I should think so," Mom said. "Stay, Nora. Believe me, it's an education watching the current generation conducting a club meeting. Anyway," she smiled, "you made the cookies. You should be around to get some of the applause."

"Well, now," Gran said, obviously pleased, "I guess I might just sit a while here in the back by the table."

She did, and Katie felt pleased, too—so different a feeling from the resentment she'd felt only weeks ago just thinking that Gran might even be in the house when the Joggers Club convened.

When the meeting finally began, Katie had no time to think about her grandmother at all, or even about why Brian Foster wasn't there, because it turned out to be a chaotic, noisy, sometimes hilarious session. They were there to try to come up with an idea for their float—a winning idea. With a theme as broad as this year's America the Beautiful, it was natural that there were lots of suggestions. From the moment Katie shouted, "I thought I said the meeting was in order!" and they all broke up laughing, nothing got back to normal. Everyone wanted to have his or her say, and everyone talked at once.

"How about a flag made out of flowers, like at the Rose Parade?"

"It's American and it's beautiful, all right. But not too original."

"Besides, where would we get all those flowers?"

"How would we pay for them if we did get them? You're talking big bucks."

"We could do those great stone faces, then. Or whatever they're called. In South Dakota—you know, those four dudes: Jefferson, Washington. We could use papier-mâché."

"Yuk!" There were groans.

"How about the space shuttle? It's even called the Columbia. That's patriotic. And I'll be one of the female astronauts," Lisa Scott said.

"Double yuk!" There were more groans. "The pits. They've got moth-eaten old space capsules at the shopping mall every other Sunday."

"Then how about the Statue of Liberty?"

"So how are we supposed to make that? More papier-mâché?"

"Nah, that's easy," one of the boys called out. "We drape a sheet on Margo Gilman, coat her with glue and spray concrete on her."

"Wow! Terrific! Mega, mega!"

"Yeah," one of the girls in the Crumb Bunch snickered, "and she's already carrying a torch."

"Now, come on, be serious," Katie said, ignoring the last remark.

"All right then, how about famous American beauties to go with the theme? Like Betsy Ross or Martha Washington . . ."

"I thought you said beauties! How about Elizabeth Taylor?"

"Too old!"

"Or Mae West."

"Gross."

"Or Miss Piggy."

"Really gross!"

"A Barbie doll, then. Ken and Barbie. In jogging suits."

"Tacky. That's tacky."

"Okay, how about American heroes, instead? Abe Lincoln or Davy Crockett . . ."

"Babe Ruth . . ."

"Mr. Spock . . ."

"Mr. Magoo . . ."

"R2D2 . . ."

"Pac-Man! I vote for Pac-Man."

"Hold it! Hold it," a serious girl called out. "Let's get back to America the Beautiful. I vote we try doing Niagara Falls; that's really beautiful."

"You've got to be kidding."

"I'm not. We could do it. We'd get a big tank of water with a pump and hide it on the back of the truck, see. . . ."

"Sure, and send Sam O'Neill over in a barrel!"

"Yay, yay!"

"Cut it out, you guys," Katie said. "You're supposed to brainstorm."

"Brainstorm!" someone whooped. "You're talking about brains with this crowd?"

"How about a circus, then? We may not have brains, but we've sure got plenty of clowns!"

"Hey, that's not such a bad idea. Mike Davis rides, you know. He could be Buffalo Bob lassoing a pony."

"Terri, you nut. Buffalo Bob is the guy your mom used to watch on TV when she was a kid. You mean Buffalo Bill."

"I mean I'm buffaloed."

"Oh, no! That's supposed to be funny?"

Katie had decided the cookies and lemonade should come at the end of the proceedings, but now the meeting seemed to have floundered, disintegrating to the point where nothing at all was being accomplished. "Okay, joggers," she said, "let's take a break. Food at the end of the room. And it had better be food for thought."

Everyone broke for the table, and Katie's grandmother, who had planned to sneak out before refreshment time, found herself surrounded. Bringing in the pitchers brimming with lemonade and chock-full of ice cubes, Katie saw clearly that not one of the young people there acted in the least as if they thought Gran was odd or old or dumb or anyone to be snubbed or laughed at. Even Margo Gilman, who arrived at this point, listened when one of the boys began asking Gran about Pearl Harbor in 1944.

"Were there still any of those wrecked battleships around, Mrs. Marshall?"

"Oh, my goodness, yes," Gran said. Her eyes seemed to look off someplace else then, and you could tell her memory was vivid. "Why, the whole hulk of the *Utah* was just yards away from my office. I'd see it every morning when the flag was raised in the square between the dock and the headquarters building.''

"The headquarters building?" The voice was respectful.

Katie said, "My grandmother was aide to the executive officer at the naval air station on Ford Island, right in the middle of Pearl Harbor.''

It really was a while then before Katie could reassemble the members of the Joggers Club. As she was waving at them and calling, "Back to business, guys!" Margo Gilman came over and handed her a note. "I almost forgot, kiddo. A message from our boy Brio. Just call me Western Union.''

There was no time for Katie to read it. She pushed it into the back pocket of her jeans, her mind briefly flashing a question: Why was Margo bringing her a note from Brian Foster? Is that where he'd been—with Margo, not training at all?

Then she realized the group was gathered once more. "Now what?" Lisa Scott said.

"Decisions," Katie said. "We've been goofing around laughing at our own jokes. . . .''

"And munching out on chocolate chips," Terri said.

"And now we've got to come up with something.''

There was a dead silence for the first time that afternoon. Finally Sam O'Neill at the back near Katie's grandmother said hopefully, "Did you ever have to make any floats in the navy, Mrs. Marshall? Like on the Fourth of July or something?"

But before Gran could answer, Margo Gilman stood up and shouted, "I've got it! The navy! World War II! Patriotism—nostalgia—the whole bit."

There were excited murmurs. Margo continued, ideas coming as she spoke. "We'll ask your grandmother for one of her old uniforms."

"Hey, no," Sam interrupted. "She should wear it herself!"

"Yay, yay! Right on!"

"Mega," Margo said. "Totally terrific. We'll put a banner at the top: Remember Pearl Harbor."

"And get some old World War II posters: Uncle Sam Needs You."

"Wow! A part for me at last!" Sam said. "I get to ride on the float after all."

Everyone laughed and began calling out ideas then. The enthusiasm was real this time, and the ideas they tossed out were not just for gags, they all added to the whole. Everyone sensed that they had something good. Even when someone pointed out that they might have a hard time getting old uniforms, their spirits weren't dampened.

"We'll have to get some help from the navy. Call the naval air station at Moffett Field. Why not? It's only five miles away."

"Oh, sure, just call the commanding officer," Mike Davis said scornfully. "Hey, admiral, how about some old uniforms, and a band, while you're at it?"

"The CO at Moffett isn't an admiral, actually; he's a captain." Everyone turned to the back of the room. It was Gran's voice.

"Sure, I can see that," Sam finally said. "They're

not going to waste any admiral on a naval air base."

"Wait a minute," Margo said, "maybe Mrs. Marshall is saying she knows this captain."

No one in the room was more surprised then than Katie Marshall to find that her grandmother had served, as she called it, with Captain St. Clair, who was now the commanding officer at Moffett Field. She hadn't seen nor heard from him in thirty-five years, "But," she said, smiling, "I think he'd remember me."

It occurred to Katie to ask her grandmother after the meeting if this Captain St. Clair was by any chance named David. But she didn't have to wait until then, because presently, carried away by the enthusiastic urgings of the entire Joggers Club, Gran went right to the telephone there in the family room, called the air station and got through to the commanding officer with the simple suggestion that his secretary tell him "Nora Randall is calling." The next thing Katie knew, her grandmother was laughing and nodding into the phone, "That's right, David, it's Nora."

Perhaps the navy would have been glad to help out the Joggers Club at Linda Vista High School in any case, just as a matter of good public relations. As it was, there was nothing the navy seemed unwilling or unable to come up with: uniforms, posters, and yes, why not the station's marching band at the head of their entry?

"Man, this is going to be some kind of float!"

This happy exclamation just about summed up everyone's feelings as they adjourned the meeting, agreeing that a committee could make final plans and assign specific jobs the following Monday.

After the last jogger left, Gran shook her head. "I think I'd better rest a little, Katie-doll." Even the pet name did not jar any longer, Katie noted. It was, well, it was just natural. It was what her grandmother called her, that's all, and it was okay, kind of nice, in fact.

Gran went out, and Katie began cleaning up but stopped when her mother came into the room and listened appreciatively to the story of the meeting. Then she said, "Now you'd better grab some studying time before dinner, dear."

It was not until she was alone in her room, sitting at her desk and resisting the temptation to turn on KOME, that Katie thought of the note in her back pocket. Brian! He hadn't come, but at least he'd sent a note, even if it arrived via Margo Gilman. Their plan was to go Sunday to Woodlands Park to find the lost gear; she assumed the note was about the time or to say, "Sorry I missed the meeting but I'll be over tonight to get your dad's permission for Sunday." Something like that.

Katie opened the note slowly and a little absently. She was concentrating on her name written on the envelope in his handwriting—just the four letters *K-A-T-E* with a kind of dashing tilt to the *K*. She liked the whole look of it. She picked up a thick, black pen from her desk and copied it on a tablet of scratch paper and then on an impulse wrote "Foster" after it. She liked the look of that, too, and wrote "Kate Foster" over ten times before she stopped, feeling foolish but happy.

At last she pulled the single sheet of white paper

out. She read what it said and then read it again.
She read it almost ten times. It was quite short. It
said:

> Kate,
> I cannot see you again. I trust you to under-
> stand. I'm sorry about our date for the park
> on Sunday. We'll just have to call it off. I'm
> sure your parents can help you find your
> things. As for running, you'll be back on your
> own Monday. At least Coach will be happy.
> > Brian.

There was an added sentence below that signa-
ture: "You are so young, Kate. If only this were
years from now." The handwriting, its jaunty slant
broken, showed that the words were written in
haste and perhaps in anguish. But Katie's eyes
were too blurry with tears to see this at all.

Katie lay awake for a long time that Thursday
night. She tried to think about the good things that
had happened that day. That was what you were
supposed to do when everything looked grim. The
float was finally planned, and it was going to be a
winner, she felt sure. Everything was all right at
last between her and her grandmother, and almost
between her and her father. After some whispering
with her mother, when she supposed Mom had told
him Katie was suffering from some tragic romance,
Dad had said gruffly as she went off to bed, "I think
you've gotten the point of this grounding, Katie.
No reason to overdo it. Why not turn over a new
leaf as of tomorrow? You'll be on your own again."

He'd concluded with a sort of fake cheerfulness. But that was okay; he meant to be doing something nice, to be comforting.

Well, she was on her own, all right. Brian had said it, and now Dad. She tried to imagine what it would be like around school. She'd be seeing Brian across campus again with all the older gang. That's how he'd avoid her. Maybe she should just hide in Poker Flats with the freshmen; that would save him the trouble. As for running, she couldn't imagine how it would be to run without him beside her. It wouldn't be the same with DeeDee; it would never be the same with anyone else again. How could he do this? He'd asked her to understand. No, he'd said he trusted her to understand. That was more than she could do, more than he should have expected of her.

Katie tried to remember what her grandmother had said. "Try to understand, Katie. He's a man, Katie-doll. . . ." All right, maybe so. And what was she supposed to be? Again the same old answer—a little girl, a kid! If she were Margo Gilman's age, his note seemed to say, it would be all right for them to see each other, to care about each other. Why didn't someone try understanding *her* feelings? How about that for a change?

But in the midst of this bitter thought Katie Marshall fell asleep, and she dreamed of Brian Foster. It was not a troubled dream at all but a beautiful one, for they were running in the sunlight on Windy Hill Trail, alone, free, in love. And they ran without tiring, turning back onto Indian Camp trail, flying along past beautiful buckeyes and fields of wild flowers. And oh, the air that flowed past them was so fresh, so pure, and suddenly in some special way so wonderfully fragrant. They stopped and were in a magic place. There was a giant branch of wild lilac, twenty feet tall, and at its top waved a glorious red banner. . . .

Katie stirred, half awake yet still in the midst of her dream. It was the scent—that scent. It was not wild lilac, it was . . . And then she was fully awake. She sat bolt upright in bed. She saw the spot where they had hidden their gear as clearly as in the dream, but more important, she knew now exactly how to go there: What she had breathed in at that magic place was the scent of bay leaf. That was it! There was a buckeye in bloom, yes, and with its splashy white blossoms that's all she and DeeDee had seen. But close by, among those oaks, there was surely a bay laurel tree. It wouldn't be hard to find. A bay tree was distinctive, both in its shape and leaf, and in the low foothills there weren't many of them. She'd find it, all right. If she didn't see it, she'd smell it; and as Katie lay back for just a moment, it seemed to her that she was once more enveloped in the aromatic fragrance of her dream.

Sometime in the course of that Friday Katie decided that she would go to Woodlands Park and get the lost gear. When she tried to sort it all out later, however, it seemed to her that she had never decided anything at all. Going to the park was suddenly just something she knew she was going to do.

School went by quickly and was not as horrible as she thought it would be, although she didn't set eyes on Brian Foster all day. Members of the Joggers Club gathered around her in the morning before class, talking excitedly about the float. In English, Miss Cummings said her report on the Great Chain of Being of Shakespeare's time was "absolutely fine, Katie—A work all the way," and Katie thought of those angels at the top of the chain, just below God, sort of running things with an iron hand. You didn't step out of line or you broke the chain, and that was disaster. When you knew so clearly where you belonged and what you were supposed to do every minute and every second, it sure must have made things easier, she thought.

When Katie found DeeDee, she broke the good news that she was no longer grounded. "I'll come over Saturday as soon as I finish what I've got to do at home. I'll hurry. You need company or you'll go stir crazy." At lunch she found a dollar bill tucked in with her sandwich and apple. A note from Gran said, "There wasn't a single chocolate chip left, Katie-doll. Buy yourself an ice cream bar," and Katie smiled. During gym Coach Miles came by and watched her run a lap and put a stopwatch on her for the next one, and she didn't mind that much. In fact she stepped up her speed and was sure she'd done the last half, 220, in fifty seconds— and that pace almost hit a 6-minute mile.

"Looking good, Marshall," he shouted. "And don't get yourself grounded anymore! Got that?"

After school, just as she came to her own house, Sam O'Neill ran past her, spun around and stopped. "I've got the running duty today," he said, and when he saw her puzzled expression, he grinned. "I mean you." When Katie asked stiffly if this was the coach's idea or Brian Foster's, Sam just shrugged. "What difference does it make? But you'd better change so we can get going. I've gotta get back to the track."

And finally, when Mom asked at dinner, "How did the day go, Katie?" she was surprised to hear her own voice saying, "Not so bad. Honest." Then she added, "It was like Dad said, I was on my own."

Katie didn't say this sarcastically or bitterly. It was just true. Was she resigned to her fate, as they wrote in those romantic novels? It didn't seem that way, for thinking of Brian Foster hurt almost too much to let it happen. She understood at last what they meant in these same books about sad ladies in distant times when they wrote something like, "She gazed out to sea with an aching heart." Katie's heart ached.

But still—and this is what she had discovered today at school—somehow you went on. You had to, and you did. And you did some good things, too, and once in a while you even smiled. In her room, when she had finished studying, Katie stayed up a while. In a way, she was still studying. She had dug out the map of Woodlands Park that DeeDee had handed her as they had ridden home in Margo Gilman's jeep, and now she had it spread out on the desk. Mileage was given for all trails, and the scale was there in the lower left corner. The one thing that Katie felt quite sure of was that they'd been going for almost five minutes on the middle trail, Indian Camp, when they had stopped to hide their warm-up suits and DeeDee's pack. If they'd

been running about a 12-minute mile, they'd have
covered slightly over one-third of a mile in five
minutes.

Fine. Katie measured off the mile, divided it into
three segments and put a big X to the left of the
black line of the trail between the second and third
segments. That's where she'd find the bay laurel
tree and the buckeye with the big rock at its base.
She could judge her pace and time herself carefully. And if she ran by, she saw from the map that
there was a small offshoot trail at exactly one-half
mile. It was drawn as a thin, very light line on the
map that went to the left doubling back southwest
near the X she had put in. It was labeled Coyote
Springs Trail, and the springs itself showed as a dot
on the map.

Katie couldn't tell from the map whether the
trail was still in use and actually marked on the
path. If it was, it was one more signpost she and
DeeDee had missed. At least it showed there was
water off that way as she had thought. The small
trail ended at a blue line that was the stream
running between Indian Camp Trail and Quarry
Basin Trail. Satisfied, Katie folded up the map and
stuck it into the back pocket of an old pair of
cut-offs. Ready for Sunday.

As she dropped off to sleep that night, Katie felt
no fear at all about the idea of going to Woodlands
Park by herself. After all, the disaster that took
place there with DeeDee was not due to any kind
of violence. They hadn't been attacked or robbed
or anything like that. The mess they got into was
strictly due to her own dumbness: She'd let them
get lost. The park itself had turned out to be a

totally safe place, as benign and friendly as the little park near her home, just lots bigger and oh, so beautiful. And the people there were just like the ones in her neighborhood, too: moms, dads, kids, young people, older ones, all running, riding, bicycling. Oh, sure, there'd been the two guys who ran up behind her and scared her half to death. But that, too, had been her own dumbness; they'd just been playing, goofing around the way the boys at LV did—or boys anywhere. Katie slept.

It was late Saturday afternoon before Katie could get to DeeDee's house. She had run early with Sam, right after he'd finished with his papers. Then she'd gone with her mother for the weekly shopping at the supermarket, unloaded the groceries, cleaned her room, then both bathrooms. After lunch she had corralled Beauty and given her a good brushing. It was not exactly an assigned task, but she usually did it every Sunday afternoon. Tomorrow she wouldn't be here. No reason to make Beauty miss their weekly ritual just because Katie had something important to do. "Lie down and hold still, Beaut," she said. "You know you love it."

Next, Katie went for her laundry bag. Doing her laundry was the last chore left except for mopping the kitchen floor, and that would have to wait because Gran was in there making strawberry tarts. Katie had picked the strawberries, too, from their own front yard, where she had to admit the fruits, vegetables and flowers all thriving together there looked great. She ducked her head into the kitchen as she started for the utility room. "I'm just throwing my dirty clothes in the washer, Gran. Why don't you hand yours over?" It had never occurred to her before, but why shouldn't she do Gran's laundry when she did her own? No problem.

By four o'clock Katie had folded and divided the laundry and had pushed the squeegee sponge mop around the kitchen floor in what she figured was a record, even for her. She walked out the back door with the mop, stood it up against the garage wall, and hollered, "I'm off to DeeDee's!" It was a shout meant for whoever heard it in the house—or next door, for that matter.

At the Ross home Katie found DeeDee sunk in gloom, unconsoled even by her kitten, Patch. Staying inside all week with her younger brother and two little sisters had taken a toll on her. She'd missed the Joggers Club meeting and was still grounded for another week. She confessed that she'd even have been glad to run five miles a day, something she'd sworn she'd never do unless forced by an ogre with a big club. Furthermore, there'd been a dual track meet at the nearby junior college today. She and Katie had planned to go. Sam was entered in both the low and high hurdles, and Brian Foster was expected to win three short races and lead his team in cross-country.

Katie had not told DeeDee about her note from Brian. She wasn't sure whether this was because it hurt too much to talk about or because keeping this hurt to herself was part of the new "being on her own" feeling she had. Thus DeeDee didn't realize that Katie would not have been going to the meet anyway. What she did decide to tell DeeDee, though, was about her dream of Thursday night, about waking up knowing just where their lost belongings were. That, she thought, would surely cheer up her friend. Maybe when Katie appeared with her clothes and her pack and, most important, her glasses, then maybe DeeDee would be able to work her way out of the doghouse. Another whole week would certainly be cruel punishment.

"You mean you think you and Brian can just run right down Indian Camp Trail, timing yourselves for four miles on that fancy watch of Brian's and then just calmly shove through the scrub brush and find it?" It was DeeDee talking to her, looking doubtful.

Katie chose her words carefully then, realizing she had to let DeeDee think she was going to the park with Brian. "All I'm saying is I know right where the spot is. You wait and see."

"Just my luck for some animal to have clumped through the underbrush and crushed my glasses," DeeDee said, not questioning Katie any further about her plans.

"Deer don't clump, DeeDee," said Katie. "Bobcats don't either, or foxes. And I really don't think there're any elephants roaming around Woodlands Park, do you? So don't worry. Your glasses won't be broken."

The confidence Katie expressed to DeeDee stayed with her, even when she awoke the next morning realizing that this was Sunday, the day she'd set for her mission. She was neither afraid nor excited. There was one moment when she wished terribly, achingly, that Brian would be going with her. But he had ended everything between them; there was just no use thinking about him. And there was another moment when she realized that she could call it all off simply by asking her dad to take her up to Woodlands and go out with her on the trail.

But Katie never considered changing her course. Bringing back the things she'd lost seemed like her own responsibility. She wanted to set things right for DeeDee and to rescue the new jacket Gran had given her the money for. Most of all she wanted to show the adults in her life—and she supposed this included Brian Foster—that she wasn't a dumb little kid who got lost and was careless with her possessions. It wasn't the same as when she'd gone off to Woodlands Park that other time with DeeDee. Then she'd been angry and impulsive and defiant. Now it seemed to her that what she proposed to do was carefully thought out and would be done for the right reasons. She was behaving like a mature person. She would be one of them.

It was in this mood, feeling pleased with herself and maybe a little self-righteous, that Katie changed her clothes after church and set off for DeeDee's. She said that's where she was going, and that's where she went. It was warm, and she had changed into her cut-offs and an old Linda Vista High T-shirt. It had the letters *LVHS* in orange scripted across the white shirt over a cartoon drawing of their goofy roadrunner mascot. Katie liked the way it looked. She didn't take anything else with her; she expected to be back easily within an hour and a half, earlier if she got rides without waiting. She almost wished she could say to DeeDee, "Okay with you if I'm here for an hour or so, in case anyone calls?" But she couldn't do that.

Instead she spent five minutes with DeeDee, saying she just wanted to check in on her but had to get going. When DeeDee said, "Where to?" Katie got vague and mumbled something about an errand. DeeDee grinned. "You can't fool me, Katie Marshall! You're going to meet Brian Foster and run, aren't you? Gee," she complained, "why didn't he just pick you up here? He could have brought Sam over." If DeeDee even thought about the park trip, she didn't mention it; she seemed to be full of her own problems. "Honest, Katie, how am I going to last out another week?"

You won't have to, DeeDee. That's the cheerful thought that went through Katie's head as she ran easily toward the corner of Oak and Plaza. *When I show up with your glasses, they'll spring you for sure!*

11

As she waited at the corner of Oak and Plaza, Katie half-wished that Mrs. Rutledge would come driving up. If you were going to hitch with a stranger for the first time in your life, Mrs. Rutledge had certainly turned out to be the very best person you could have stop for you. But of course, no Mrs. Rutledge appeared. Instead a young couple slowed and the woman called through the window, "We're headed for Woodlands Park," and when Katie called back, "Me too," they drew up to the curb.

There were two bikes on a rack at the back of the car, and they had a baby, a little girl about a year old, Katie guessed, sitting between them in a car seat. Katie climbed into the back seat, relieved that her initial step had been taken so easily. She should have guessed what the first bit of conversation would be. The young mother turned to her and said, "You're not going up to spend a day in Woodlands all by yourself, are you?"

Katie told a fib, or a partial fib, and mentally apologized. "I'm meeting a gang that's already up there," she said. "I had to wait until church was over."

"Of course," the woman said.

"I dunno," the man said, talking more to his wife than to her. "I don't think I'll let this one hitch by herself while she's still in high school." He must have seen her T-shirt.

"No way," the woman said, shaking her head earnestly. "Not our little girl." But then she smiled back at Katie. "Don't you worry about us, though, we're safe as can be." Katie nodded, and the woman went on. "I see you go to Linda Vista. That's where Chuck and I went to high school, too."

"Yeah, and don't tell her when," her husband said, laughing. "It's like a thousand years ago. I guess we're old folks now." He sighed, but really it seemed to Katie that they were happy enough and lucky, too, to be driving out to the park in their little car with bikes and a baby and a picnic basket.

She left them at the park gate assembling their bicycles, the father adding a little seat for the baby on the back of his. "Thanks again," she called. "Maybe I'll see you on the trails."

Katie looked at her watch as she headed out on the main trail. She had always made fun of stop-watches, but today she wished she had one. But she'd run with DeeDee almost every day for a long time, and she could pick up their pace easily enough; so for time, her old watch would just have to do. Five minutes then. It was exactly 12:05.

She came quickly to the place where the trail divided into three and took the middle fork straight ahead of her without even breaking her stride. She was on Indian Camp Trail just as she should be and had the path to herself. There didn't seem to be anyone else out at all. She supposed most people were already settled at picnic tables, or if they'd come to run, they'd have been there hours ago and gone home. She kept expecting the young people to wheel by any second on their bikes. They certainly wouldn't choose Windy Hill Trail, though they might have gone down Quarry Basin, she supposed.

Suddenly Katie realized there was someone close behind her. She could hear breathing, heavy and uneven. He wasn't a runner; she instantly knew that, and he hadn't come along the path at all; she knew that, too. He must have come through the scrub brush alongside the trail just after she went by. Had he been waiting for someone—for her? Katie started to increase her speed, for the breathing was close now. But she was overcome with a sudden terror, a fear much greater than that other time when the two young men had overtaken her. This was different, this was for real.

She had to get away, her legs had to work! She willed herself to speed, willed her body to respond. Still she heard the breathing close behind her— closer . . . closer. She stretched out her legs, and a voice said, "No you don't, girlie," and for the briefest moment she had the sense that someone had reached for her T-shirt and missed.

Katie took off. "No you don't," she heard again.

Yes I do! He'd never catch her, he wouldn't!

She rounded a wide bend in the trail and went even faster. She realized she must be close to the *X* on the map that marked the lost gear, but she couldn't slow now to catch sight of a bay tree or a buckeye. She had to keep going, to get far away, to find help. Where were all the people? Where *were* they? *I've got to hide,* she thought, *but where?*

Then the map of Woodlands Park, the whole spread-out face of it, flashed across her mind as if on a giant screen. She saw her own big *X* mark and just beyond it the little line that veered left. Coyote Springs Trail. It had to be there almost right now. Turn left. Left! She saw an opening just ahead and careened off the wide main trail.

She was on a much smaller path then, and as she ran, it narrowed even more, and she found that her head and shoulders were breaking through chaparral that almost made a tunnel of the trail. She felt the stickiness of blood from scratches, and once her T-shirt caught and she nearly screamed aloud thinking for one awful moment that the sudden grab had come from a human source. She tore away from the branch and pushed on.

She was still running, though much slower as the brush at each side of the trail became even thicker. She knew that the path had turned and twisted as she ran, but she was sure she was still on it. She could see the map and the way Coyote Springs Trail curved around until it finally made a U-turn and ran parallel to Indian Camp between her *X* and the stream. She thought she heard water, turned to her right toward the sound and the force of her body, still moving, carried her in that direction, crashing against the brush. Then, with no warning, the chaparral that seemed so thick gave way, and Katie fell headlong into an opening, hitting a stone as she went down.

She lay there a moment, panting. She wasn't dead, that was certain. She could feel blood against her cheek. She started to pull herself up, then felt a sharp twinge of pain. Her left ankle. It was caught; it hurt. Gingerly she rolled over on her back, hoisted herself on one arm and looked. Her ankle was trapped by a pair of manzanita branches that formed a neat, tight *V* at the base.

Okay, she thought, I can pull the dumb thing out of there. The ankle, hanging limp, didn't really seem like part of her—until she tried to move it again and involuntarily cried out.

"Ouch!" she heard herself say and then dropped back flat, terrified. *I've made a noise,* she thought. *Oh, please don't let him find me!*

She lay absolutely still then, listening, concentrating with all her might on the environment around her. She could hear the water that had attracted her and from the sounds knew it was the springs, not the creek. All else was quiet in the early afternoon sun, except for the ongoing scratching sounds of a bird. She moved her head gently, slowly, and saw a brown thrush not three feet away. The bird was somehow a comfort. Seeing it so close at hand, hearing it go about its business unconcerned, made her feel safe.

Cautiously Katie sat up again. She was conscious of the blood wet on her face. She felt the source and found a knob on her forehead, just at the hairline. There the blood was beginning to thicken. It would soon dry and cake. As best she could, using the front of her T-shirt, Katie wiped her face and dabbed at her forehead. Then she leaned forward and carefully, using both hands, lifted her ankle off the crotch of the manzanita bush.

The ankle was beginning to swell. She poked it a bit, wanted to holler "ouch" again but didn't. She decided it wasn't broken, just sprained. She looked at her watch. It was now 2:30. She should begin to move toward help. She was sure by now she had lost her pursuer. If he'd turned off onto Coyote Springs Trail, she'd have heard him, all right—and he her.

Okay, she thought, first things first. Can I walk?

She got to her feet, hoisting herself up by pulling on the bushes, and discovered then that there was no way she was going to be able to put weight on her left foot. She looked around her; she couldn't see the trail she'd gone off at all, but on the far side of the tiny pocket clearing where she was she could see the springs. Okay, she'd get to them, clean off her wound and the scratches on her legs, take a good long drink and then figure out what next.

Because she could not climb or even shove her way through the chaparral, Katie got down on her hands and knees and crawled. It was a three-legged crawl, really; she simply dragged her left leg. But she got there, washed, dunked her whole head under the water that ran down the rocks and then let the cool springs run over her ankle. At last she sat back against a young redwood tree. She was alone at Coyote Springs; not even any coyotes around, not until nightfall. Her ankle was terribly swollen by now. Gross, she thought, really gross. And it throbbed. So did her head, she realized. But she felt oddly peaceful as she sat there, and a little light-headed. She told herself she must decide whether to wait where she was and hope someone would check out every trail for her or drag herself somehow back to the main trail. She should decide, yet it was so nice here by the springs. She would decide later.

Presently Katie Marshall dropped off to sleep with the soothing sounds of water rippling over rocks and filling her ears.

It was five o'clock when Katie woke up. She was instantly alert. Almost like a young animal she laid still and made sure of what was going on around her before she moved. She felt stupid to have slept. If someone had come along the trail, she could have called to them. Now it was late afternoon. The park gates closed at seven. She didn't want to spend the night alone. She must find help. Realistically she understood that no one would be out looking for her yet. It would be just about now, in fact, that her mother would call DeeDee and say, "DeeDee, dear, you'd better tell Katie to come along home." She could imagine Mom's reaction when DeeDee said, "Gee, Mrs. Marshall, Katie left here ages ago."

Well, DeeDee would have to use her brains and figure out where Katie was. "Come on, DeeDee," she said to herself, "remember how I told you about knowing just where our stuff was, about the bay tree? You know me; you can guess where I am."

DeeDee would tell them. They'd come for her, that was for sure. In the meantime she'd better use *her* brains and make it easy for them. She understood now that Coyote Springs Trail was a thin little line on the map because it just wasn't a trail at all anymore. No one was keeping it up; the turnoff from Indian Camp Trail wasn't even marked. She had better get back on the main trail.

She got up. "Never mind that your stupid head hurts like the dickens," she said to herself, "just see if you can move with this ankle." But her ankle was too swollen and now so stiff it was of no use whatsoever. She would have to crawl again, drag herself. She'd never get back to the place where this trail joined Indian Camp again. It must be almost a mile with all the turns it made. For the only moment since she had fallen that afternoon, Katie felt despair.

It was exactly then that the Woodlands Park trail map fell from the pocket of her jeans. It was a signal, as if someone had dropped a message in her lap. She didn't even need to look at the map. She knew what its message was: At the point where she was now Coyote Springs Trail was running parallel to Indian Camp Trail, and the little springs itself was directly back of the big *X* she had marked. Okay, all she had to do was cross through the chaparral, she judged, get up a slope and she would come to the rock, the lilac branch, the red headband itself, probably on the ground. She smiled to herself. Maybe that's what she'd see first; after all, she'd be crawling. No, if she kept her head up, what she'd see first would be the bay tree. She knew it was there. She began to move in that direction.

Katie had accurately reconstructed the scene at the Marshall home around five o'clock and also the telephone conversation with DeeDee at the Ross home. But at this point she had oversimplified: When it was clear Katie wasn't at her own house or DeeDee's, DeeDee did not think of Woodlands Park and the bay tree at all. She thought of her own remark, "I'll bet you're going to meet Brian Foster and run."

In the part of her that had been Katie Marshall's best friend since they were five years old, DeeDee couldn't believe Katie had really gone off somewhere with Brian without telling her parents. But in another part of her, DeeDee recognized a newer Katie and understood that she might just possibly have done exactly that. Reluctantly DeeDee told Katie's mother they'd better telephone Brian Foster's home if they were really worried, although she added loyally, "I think she'll show up any minute, Mrs. Marshall. Honest. Like, she might sort of have, you know, just forgotten the time."

Katie's father telephoned the Foster home. Brian answered. He had not seen Katie, he said. It was clear he was telling the truth. Mr. Marshall tried to sound offhand; he'd phone around to Katie's friends, he said. Probably she was doing homework with someone or maybe had gone over to the track at school to run with a friend. But Brian Foster knew how Mr. Marshall felt; he felt the same way.

"May I come over, sir?" he asked. "I'll stop by the Ross's on the way. Maybe DeeDee can remember something else Kate said that would give us a clue."

It gave Katie's father a start to hear his daughter called Kate. *They grow up so fast,* he thought, *there's so little time to know them. Katie, Kate.* And while his wife went about making calls, he put himself to comforting his own mother. Katie's grandmother was trying to quiet Beauty, Katie's dog, for like all dogs she knew and had known instantly that something was wrong. But now Mr. Marshall could see that Gran herself was distraught. And so there he was with his arm around his mother when Brian Foster's old Mustang wheeled into their drive, the top down as always. It seemed to Mr. Marshall that Brian was out of the car and at their front door before the motor had stopped.

"We're sure she's at Woodlands Park, Mr. Marshall," he said. "We'll have to get right out there or the gates will be closed." He explained about the dream, the bay tree, the hiding place.

Mr. Marshall was nodding. "We'd better take flashlights. It'll get dark about seven."

"I'll stay with Gran, dear," Mrs. Marshall said to her husband. She gave his arm a squeeze. She wished she could go, but she knew it was her place to be with Katie's grandmother. "Luck, dear, luck."

"We'll find her, Mrs. Marshall." It was Brian

looking at her fiercely, his blue eyes ablaze with emotion. *Why*, she thought, *he cares for Katie.* She caught Gran's eyes, and the two women exchanged a look; Gran understood, too.

"I know you will, Brian," Mrs. Marshall said, and then added involuntarily to her husband, "It's such a big place, John."

"Yes, but Katie knew exactly where she was going, and it's not more than a half-mile in," Mr. Marshall said firmly. And then stopped. For it struck them all then: If Katie had left DeeDee's home before noon and had only a short way to go in the park and still was not back, then something must have happened to her. But what? Lost? Hurt? Kidnapped?

"Katie-doll!" It was Gran calling out Katie's name, but she did not cry, and it was Gran who said to the two men as they went out the door, "Take Beauty," and the old dog understood and ran to the back of the station wagon and jumped in the way she used to when she was a pup and the family went off picnicking together.

"That's right, Beauty. Good girl!" Katie's father said and for just a moment looked a little less grim. "We'll go find Katie."

At the park an employee had just arrived to close the gates. He said he could radio for help from his pickup truck, but Brian Foster already had Beauty on her leash and was starting off up the main trail, running. "Hold off," he called. "We'll find her. It won't be five minutes."

The man shrugged. "I hope he's right, mister," he said to Mr. Marshall.

"I hope so, too," Mr. Marshall said. "I'd be grateful if you'd wait until we come out, though."

"Sure thing. I'll be right here in my truck."

Mr. Marshall set off, but although he ran at what seemed a good pace to him and even turned on his flashlight in the gathering nightfall, he didn't catch even a glimpse of Brian Foster. But then he heard Beauty—a tremendous, excited, insistent barking. He slowed and smiled. They'd found her—and in less than three minutes.

But all Brian Foster had found as he followed Beauty off the trail through the chaparral was the hiding place with all their gear. It was Katie's clothes that had led Beauty so unerringly to the spot, snuffling at the rock, digging, triumphantly uncovering the lost jacket, still bright and blue in the shine of Brian's flashlight. Brian's heart sank as he swept his light around the small clearing, saw the buckeye with its white plumes, found the bay tree, too. She had been right; it was there, close by, growing between two oaks just where the land sloped off sharply. But Katie Marshall was not there.

"Kate," he said softly. "Kate, darling, where are you?"

It had seemed so easy; he had been so sure of her. She would have come to this place. Beauty was still barking, wagging her tail, waiting for approval. "Yes," he said, "good dog, Beaut. You found Katie's jacket." Then he knelt down beside the dog and put his arms around her. "But you see, Beaut, we must find Kate. Find Kate," he repeated, and then called as loudly as he could. "Kate!"

"Here. I'm right here."

It was over then. And Brian had been right: It had not taken more than five minutes from the park gates to the moment he knelt beside Katie and took her in his arms.

It had all happened so fast at that moment when he heard her voice, weak, but clear. Beauty had torn from her leash and gone over the slope in back of the two oak trees and the bay. Brian had directed his flashlight down into the shallow ravine and caught the white T-shirt and then the waving stick with a circlet of red at the top just as Beauty came into the light. He'd half-run and half-leaped to reach her side, and then he'd held her as her words tumbled out in those few minutes before her father arrived.

"I couldn't make it the last part of the way, Brian, up that bank, even though I could smell the bay tree, just like in my dream, but I couldn't make it. I had to lie back and wait, and then I saw the stick. It must have been dragged down here by a deer, and I thought I'd wave it and someone would see. But then I knew it would be dark soon and no one would ever find me—I was so scared." He hugged her, and she shook her head. "You see, I suddenly thought of DeeDee's joke. She said the red headband on the stick was like marking a new grave." He pulled her head to his chest and cradled it gently. "But I knew you would come. Oh, no, not you; I never thought of that—though once I think I fell asleep and dreamed it, just like this." He kissed her forehead where it was cut while Beauty licked scratches on her legs. She sighed, "I heard you right away—I mean, I heard Beauty. But I didn't recognize her bark. Everything sounded so different down here—or maybe it's just that I was so scared I thought it might be someone else, that I shouldn't make a sound. And then I heard a voice calling, 'Kate.'" She raised her head and looked Brian Foster straight in the eyes. "It was you, Brian."

Then she felt suddenly shy and lowered her head, but he tipped it back up to his. "I was wrong, Kate. About us. Forgive me. I was so afraid of my feelings—of our feelings. I should have trusted you. I should never have cut you off. I never will again."

Tenderly then he kissed her full on the mouth, and she did not feel shy anymore, nor afraid, but felt only a freedom and a warmth, a kind of running away of her heart, as if it embraced all of Woodlands Park: Windy Hill, Indian Camp, Coyote Springs—all of it. And Brian Foster.

12

One week later Katie Marshall was once more at the intersection of Oak and Plaza in Linda Vista, that fateful corner where she had twice come to set out on forbidden adventures. But this Saturday she did not arrive in a furtive fashion at a deserted bus stop. Instead, Katie arrived with her parents, joining hundreds of other families and neighbors who had come for the gala Linda Vista homecoming parade. What set her apart from the others was twofold: She was on her way to a special roped-off section in the grandstand erected along one block of the Plaza Street sidewalk, for Katie was to be a parade judge. And she was making her way to this honored seat slowly, limping conspicuously, aided by a sturdy cane.

There was a story about that cane—and about the large chrome watch she glanced at self-consciously as she took a seat between the mayor of Linda Vista, Mr. Henderson, and the chairman of the parade committee, who turned out to be, to Katie's delight, none other than Mrs. Rutledge, her first chauffeur up to Woodlands Park. Mrs. Rutledge accepted without question Katie's truthful explanation of her strapped ankle as a running accident, and Katie's parents, sitting just behind her in the stands, added not a word as Katie introduced them. When Mrs. Rutledge admired the carved lion's head on Katie's cane, Katie said, "My grandmother gave me this cane."

Gran handing Katie the cane the night she was brought home from the park was just one of the wonderful things that had happened that Sunday evening. A stop at the hospital emergency room had shown she had a slight concussion and a badly sprained ankle. It was not broken, and that was good, although Katie seriously heeded the young doctor's warning that for a runner a sprain could be worse than a small break because it meant ligaments were torn. She knew she must be very careful to heal well, for running was surely going to become an increasingly important part of her life. She knew that.

"Off your feet as much as possible and good support when you do move around," the doctor had said. And when this instruction was reported in the family room at 45 Ivy Lane that night, Gran had simply handed Katie her cane.

"I don't need it anymore," she said, and as they all watched, astonished, she calmly walked across the room to the kitchen door. "We old navy types are pretty rugged, you know," she added. "You don't think I'm going to represent the United States Navy on a float in the Linda Vista homecoming parade hanging onto some cane like a worn-out old battleship, do you?"

Then DeeDee had called, grateful for her glasses, but most of all glad that Katie was safe, and Sam was on the line, too, saying, "Hey, look, Katie, I'll ride you to school on the back of my bike every day." Coach Miles had called and was very gruff, giving her far more orders about what to do for her ankle than the young doctor. Then the doorbell had rung at nine o'clock, and in came the last person Katie expected to see—Margo Gilman, looking as provocative as ever in red shorts and a bare midriff sweat shirt top.

"Just driving by in the old jeep," she had said casually. "Thought I'd check you out. We need you for that float, kiddo." Strangely, the way she said "kiddo" didn't grate at all on Katie; it was as if she meant to signal that they were friends. Then she had turned to Brian Foster, who still sat with his arm around Katie, and said, "Take care of Katie, Brio, old friend, and get her to the float on time." And then she was gone, leaving Katie and Brian alone in the family room.

Brian had taken her left hand and gently pulled off her old wristwatch. "I'm not sure you're going to make that float, Kate, but you should be able to check the time properly when you start running again." He unstrapped his huge, chrome pilot's watch, the chronograph with its three dials, and fastened it around her wrist. Katie's mother came into the room and said quietly, "I think Katie should get to bed now, Brian, don't you?"

"You're right, Mrs. Marshall. I'll just carry her in if that's all right with you."

That's the kind of night it had been, with Gran smiling and stealing in to kiss her, and Beauty sleeping, unscolded, beside her bed. Even Dad poked his head in to say he'd drive her to school, but he'd said right away, "Sounds good to me," when she told him Brian Foster was going to pick her up. "And about today at the park, Katie," he added, "I can see you thought you were doing a good thing. You found out you were wrong. That's what's important to your mother and me—that and the fact that you're here, home safe. 'Nuff said."

He left the room, and Katie went to sleep with the hard face of the big watch against her cheek, the sound of its ticking in her ear.

It was Coach Miles who arranged for Katie to be a judge for the homecoming parade. There was always one student included to represent the high school. As President of the Joggers Club, she was a good choice, he insisted, and if she ended up voting for the club's float, well, they'd just have to assume that meant it was, in fact, number one.

Now Katie sat in the reviewing stand, determined to do her duty properly but so full of excitement she could hardly contain herself. She was wearing a summer dress that had a full skirt and an open neck with a small ruffle that came down to her waist. It was the softest, airiest, lightest color of blue, and she loved wearing it. Around her shoulders she had tied a loose, cable-knit sweater in three shades of blue, and at her throat she wore a single, flat, narrow silver chain, chosen to go with the chrome watch on her wrist.

Katie had not seen the Joggers Club float; they had all said they wanted her to be surprised. She'd just found out the club's parade position from the program list handed her by the mayor: It would be the last in line. She'd have to wait to see them all—Gran, DeeDee, Sam, and of course, Brian. She heard the strains of a band strike up. The street was empty, but she knew they were all there massed in formation around the corner on Oak. The band went through a practice run of the Linda Vista fight song and scattered voices joined in:

> Linda Vista, Linda Vista,
> Play with all your might!
> Win the game, the glory and fame
> For dear old orange and white.
> Fight, fight, fight . . .

Then the music stopped and there was a kind of hush. A bugle sounded, and around the corner came the color guard from the United States Naval Air Station, Moffett Field, followed by the entire membership of Troop 957, Boy Scouts of America. And as they started by the stands, the Linda Vista High School marching band, in full dress uniform with orange plumes atop their shako hats and cheerleaders and pompon girls escorting them, broke into a rendition of "America the Beautiful." Katie stood up, leaning on her cane, and sang.

". . . And crown thy good with brotherhood from sea to shining sea."

They finished just as the queen and her court came into view riding in two white Cadillac convertibles. The queen, wearing a white satin evening dress almost like a wedding gown and a crown of white carnations, sat on the back of the seat, waving graciously to the stands with a silver scepter. It was Margo Gilman. At her side, her prince consort, sat Coach Dusty Miles in white slacks and a blue blazer, its pocket sporting an embroidered patch from his university days. Standing near the top of the stands as she was, Katie laughed to see Coach Miles's feet on the seat of the white car: He had on his favorite old, worn running shoes, laces untied.

The slow-moving convertibles drew to a stop. "Hey, hey, Margo babe!" a boy in the stands called out. "Looking good up there!" he shouted as she bowed low to the judges. And she did look good, Katie thought.

Everyone had known Margo would be elected homecoming queen. At one time Katie might have been envious, even though only seniors were eligible. But when the election results were announced over the school loudspeaker last Monday morning, Katie's first response had been, "Great—she'll make a great queen."

Those were her words to DeeDee, and when her friend said, "Great? Margo Gilman? I thought you loathed her," Katie heard herself saying, "Oh, I don't know. Margo's okay. She just thinks she has to act big sometimes. Like a little kid." It was not really her thought, it was Brian's; she knew that. But she'd made it her own, and that was a good feeling.

Today she recognized how beautiful Margo looked sitting in that white convertible, and she clapped with all the others when Mrs. Rutledge signaled to three little girls at the foot of the stands and they ran out to the car and placed an immense bouquet of American Beauty roses in Margo Gilman's arms as the white car began to move.

The parade progressed slowly. There were sixteen floats in all and two other bands, along with a troop of eight-year-old baton-twirlers from a local school and a trio of clowns who handed out balloons to anyone on the sidelines who reached for one. Mr. Marshall climbed down and brought Katie a huge, powder blue one that matched her dress. She wound it around her wrist and went on faithfully taking notes on each float, assigning ratings to each on a one-to-ten scale. Sloan's shoe store had a lowly Cinderella being fitted with a glass slipper by a handsome Prince Charming. The slipper was undoubtedly plastic, but it sparkled in the sun like crystal. Katie gave the float a ten for execution but only a two for theme. Then came the Rotary Club with its American Flag done in flowers, just as someone at the Joggers Club meeting had suggested. It was gorgeous. It got a ten for theme and execution both on Katie's list but only a two for originality.

When the Mel's Stop and Shop float arrived—they were now at number fourteen—Katie thought it was sure to be the hands-down winner on anyone's list, even over the covered wagon from the Car Club and the marvelous Lincoln–Douglas debate staged by the Drama Club, with Mike Davis looking just like Honest Abe in a black beard and

stovepipe hat. But here came the back of a truck
set up like an old-fashioned ice cream parlor with
wire-backed chairs and round tables at which children and teenagers sat dressed in 1890's costumes.
Best of all, there was a wonderful real soda foun-
tain at one end, behind which Mr. Martin, the
owner, and his son Danny dispensed real ice cream
cones and root beer floats and even, Katie noted
enviously, hot fudge sundaes. Naturally she giggled
when Mrs. Rutledge leaned over and said to her,
"Oh my, Katie, doesn't that look scrumptuous! I do
believe Mel Martin is making a strawberry ice
cream soda. If he gave it to me, I know I'd rate him
tens across the board!"

Mrs. Rutledge had to raise her voice to finish her
sentence, for the sounds of another band swelled
over the stands. It was playing "Anchors Aweigh,"
and when it appeared, wheeling perfectly around
the corner of Oak onto Plaza, Katie rose with the
rest of the spectators to watch and cheer. It was the
entire eighty-five-member band of the Moffett
Field Naval Air Station, and they were attired in
the old World War II navy uniforms, the classic
white sailor suits: bell-bottom trousers, blouses
with their wide collars and black silk ties and white
sailor caps jammed on at rakish angles.

The impact of this stirring band was hardly fair to
entry number fifteen, marching just in front of it. It
was a small float entitled, "America at Peace with
Its Neighbors": A Canadian Royal Mountie, a
Mexican hat dancer and an American trapper kept
milling about and shaking hands with one another,
and Katie guessed that the other figure standing on

a box and waving his arms over them was intended to be Father Junipero Serra, for he had on a long, brown bathrobe with a rope tied around his middle. Conscientiously Katie made herself follow this little group all the way past the stands, smiling at them and waving encouragement. She sat down then and bent over her notes to mark her ratings.

Thus it was that Katie Marshall missed the first appearance of the final float in the parade: number sixteen, entered by the Joggers Club of Linda Vista High School. But then she heard increasing cheers and stood again with her cane. Moving toward them behind the navy band, an extraordinary sight came into view. An aircraft carrier approached, its flat flight deck slanted out over its sides, its island looming high on the starboard. "U.S.S. *Enterprise*" was lettered on its prow.

Of course, the ship was made of plywood painted gray and the island superstructure was a pile of painted boxes—and all of it no more the size of a real carrier than a tugboat would be. But it filled the main street of the town of Linda Vista, and it was a brave sight. No one would have disagreed with the banner that waved from the stern reading, "The Big E," and although the bridge of this gallant ship was small, on it stood two glorious figures in navy dress whites: a captain and a navy WAVE, saluting the stands as they came abreast.

A lump came into Katie's throat, for it was Gran, of course, looking about twenty-one years old, Katie thought, and she guessed the tall man beside her must be Captain David St. Clair, the commanding officer of the air base. The way he

looked was commanding, all right, and Katie was
sure he wasn't just someone dressed up in a
costume to ride a float in a small-town parade.

She waved her cane at Gran and felt so proud
she could hardly stand it. "That's my grandmother,
Nora Marshall," she said to Mrs. Rutledge. "She
was a full lieutenant in World War II, stationed at
Pearl Harbor."

"Doesn't she look wonderful!" Mrs. Rutledge
smiled.

Katie smiled back. "I sure do think so," she said.
Then she turned her attention to the oh's and ah's
of the crowd and saw the object of their admira-
tion: On the plywood deck of this little carrier
replica, almost filling it, was a real World War II
fighter plane—a Grumman F4F Wildcat, single
wing, propeller and all, looking every bit as tough
and pugnacious as it had in the days it fought
Japanese Zeros in 1942 in the skies of the South
Pacific. There was a pilot in its cockpit, too, in a
leather helmet and goggles, looking more like
Snoopy as the Red Baron than a World War II ace.
But that was all right; you could take a lot of
liberties with a holiday float. After all, the real
Enterprise would have had its number, not its
name, on its hull, and there wouldn't have been
women on board, not in World War II. It didn't
matter, though; when the pilot of the Wildcat got
up and pulled a huge poster out of the cockpit,
people laughed and clapped at the same time. It
was the famous figure in a top hat and white beard,
pointing at the stands and saying, "Uncle Sam
Needs YOU!" and of course it was Sam O'Neill
grinning as he accepted applause.

Katie clapped wildly. How good she felt. She was there, "on her own," a judge for the homecoming parade. But she was also in Linda Vista, the town where she belonged, with her mother and father sitting just behind her and all the things she cared about out there in front of her. The whole parade was like seeing her life pass in review; every part of it meant something to her, from the high school band to the ice cream parlor, from Coach Miles to Lieutenant Nora Marshall. Only one important figure had not yet passed before her eyes, but of course, Brian Foster must be there on the U.S.S. *Enterprise* somewhere.

Then Katie heard through a microphone the very words from the poster. "Uncle Sam Needs YOU!" came through loud and clear. The long float was almost past the reviewing stand now, and Katie saw that there was a crowd of little children grouped on the broad part of the flight deck where it was built out over the end of the truck. They all wore old-fashioned white navy caps, just like the band. Sitting at a small desk behind a sign that said "U.S. Navy Recruiting Center" was her best friend DeeDee Ross wearing the gray summer uniform of a World War II WAVE. At her side, in the dress whites of a midshipman, was the man with the microphone. He was bending over the side of the truck—or more correctly, the side of the ship— facing the crowd on the other side of the street.

"Join the navy and see the world," he called out. "Come right aboard and sign up with Chief Petty Officer DeeDee Ross. If you are under ten, get your parents' permission. Boys and girls both welcome; this is an equal opportunity outfit. Everyone

who enlists will receive a World War II navy cap
absolutely free. Step right up—it's better than cap
day at the ball park!"

Of course, Katie should have recognized his
voice, even through a microphone, but she didn't,
and it was not until Brian Foster turned around,
grinning as he reached for two children who were
clambering up the "gangplank" at the rear of the
truck, that Katie Marshall knew who he was. How
marvelous he looked in his whites with the shoulder boards and the officer's hat with the gold
midshipman's anchor on the emblem. And how he
was enjoying himself as he put caps on the heads of
the two children and shook their hands. "We've got
room for more on board," he urged. "Who's next?
Don't delay! We sail in five minutes for our first
port of call—Mel's Stop and Shop float just ahead.
Every enlistee will receive his due ration of ice
cream cones."

Children were lined up now to come aboard.
Captain St. Clair came down from the bridge and
took over the microphone. Addressing the judges
in the reviewing stand, he gave a graceful little
speech in which he said that being in Linda Vista
for such an occasion made him realize the true
meaning of America the Beautiful. He thanked
them all for inviting their neighbors, the navy, to
participate in their holiday, but he gave full credit
for "this fine entry" to the Joggers Club of Linda
Vista High School. "It was their idea, and they did
it all," he said. "They wouldn't even let me have a
squadron of Tomcats fly over."

All the while Captain St. Clair was speaking,
Katie was trying to pay attention but couldn't keep

her eyes from Brian Foster. Busy playing his part as a navy recruiter, he had not even been able to look her way. But the moment the captain took the microphone from his hands, Brian had eyes only for her. It seemed to her that they were talking together over the few yards of distance between them. And laughing. For Brian was laughing now and waving at her.

And suddenly she heard her name, too. "Kate Marshall." It was the captain's voice. "And I understand the president of your Joggers Club is sitting in the stands right now—Kate Marshall." So Brian must have told him her name. And it seemed surely the right name, too, not so much that Katie, or even Katie-doll, were gone, for they would always be part of her; but they were one now, and that one was Kate Marshall.

"So if the beautiful young lady in the blue dress will accept our invitation . . ." What was he saying? ". . . we'd like to have her aboard." The captain saluted her, then turned to Brian. "Midshipman Foster," he said, "since Miss Marshall is temporarily disabled and cannot jog up here, will you escort her to the deck of the *Enterprise?*"

It was an order. Brian Foster jumped off the truck, and to the delight of the crowd, ran up the aisle of the small grandstand, made his way to Kate and, in front of them all, kissed her. "Let's go, Kate," he said, grinning. Her mother smiled, her dad winked, Mrs. Rutledge murmured, "How very nice," and the mayor harrumphed, "Take good care of her, young man." And then Kate Marshall was being helped down the steps, Brian's arm firmly around her.

"Please cast my votes, Mrs. Rutledge," Katie turned and called back, and then went on toward the funny, lovely plywood float, which surely had won her vote for the best of everything. And she was to be a queen after all, with her prince at her side, and they would ride in a coach together through the crowds of adoring subjects. The coach was a plywood aircraft carrier. No matter. Like most dreams, this one, too, had come true in a way that was different from the fantasies of her sleep, yet totally recognizable.

She went up the ramp to the float. The band struck up, and the parade began to move. Brian held her close to his side, and she felt his lips brush her hair. She slipped the round, blue balloon off her wrist and watched as it floated up into skies, which were even bluer. And Katie knew that although the parade would soon be over, her own life had just begun.

Four exciting First Love from Silhouette romances yours for 15 days—_free!_

If you enjoyed this First Love from Silhouette,® you'll want to read more! These are true-to-life romances about the things that matter most to you now—your friendships, dating, getting along in school, and learning about yourself. The stories could really happen, and the characters are so real they'll seem like friends.

Now you can get 4 First Love from Silhouette romances to look over for 15 days—absolutely free! If you decide not to keep them, simply return them and pay nothing. But if you enjoy them as much as we believe you will, keep them and pay the invoice enclosed with your trial shipment. You'll then become a member of the First Love from Silhouette℠ Book Club and will receive 4 more new First Love from Silhouette romances every month. You'll always be among the first to get them, and you'll never miss a new title. There is no minimum number of books to buy and you can cancel at any time. To receive your 4 books, mail the coupon below today.

First Love from Silhouette® is a service mark and a registered trademark of Simon & Schuster.

This offer expires March 31, 1984

 First Love from Silhouette Book Club, Dept. FL-016
120 Brighton Road, P.O. Box 5020, Clifton, NJ 07015

Please send me 4 First Love from Silhouette romances to keep for 15 days, absolutely _free_. I understand I am not obligated to join the First Love from Silhouette Book Club unless I decide to keep them.

NAME_____
(Please print)

ADDRESS_____

CITY_____ STATE_____ ZIP_____

Signature_____
(If under 18, parent or guardian must sign)

First Love from Silhouette

THERE'S NOTHING QUITE AS SPECIAL AS A <u>FIRST LOVE.</u>

$1.75 each

2 ☐ GIRL IN THE ROUGH
Wunsch

3 ☐ PLEASE LET ME IN
Beckman

4 ☐ SERENADE
Marceau

6 ☐ KATE HERSELF
Erskine

7 ☐ SONGBiRD
Enfield

14 ☐ PROMISED KISS
Ladd

15 ☐ SUMMER ROMANCE
Diamond

16 ☐ SOMEONE TO LOVE
Bryan

17 ☐ GOLDEN GIRL
Erskine

18 ☐ WE BELONG TOGETHER
Harper

19 ☐ TOMORROW'S WISH
Ryan

20 ☐ SAY PLEASE!
Francis

$1.95 each

24 ☐ DREAM LOVER
Treadwell

26 ☐ A TIME FOR US
Ryan

27 ☐ A SECRET PLACE
Francis

29 ☐ FOR THE LOVE OF LORI
Ladd

30 ☐ A BOY TO DREAM ABOUT
Quinn

31 ☐ THE FIRST ACT
London

32 ☐ DARE TO LOVE
Bush

33 ☐ YOU·AND ME
Johnson

34 ☐ THE PERFECT FIGURE
March

35 ☐ PEOPLE LIKE US
Haynes

36 ☐ ONE ON ONE
Ketter

37 ☐ LOVE NOTE
Howell

First Love from Silhouette

38 ☐ ALL-AMERICAN GIRL
Payton

39 ☐ BE MY VALENTINE
Harper

40 ☐ MY LUCKY STAR
Cassiday

41 ☐ JUST FRIENDS
Francis

42 ☐ PROMISES TO COME
Dellin

43 ☐ A KNIGHT TO REMEMBER
Martin

44 ☐ SOMEONE LIKE
JEREMY VAUGHN
Alexander

45 ☐ A TOUCH OF LOVE
Madison

46 ☐ SEALED WITH A KISS
Davis

47 ☐ THREE WEEKS OF LOVE
Aks

48 ☐ SUMMER ILLUSION
Manning

49 ☐ ONE OF A KIND
Brett

50 ☐ STAY, SWEET LOVE
Fisher

51 ☐ PRAIRIE GIRL
Coy

52 ☐ A SUMMER TO REMEMBER
Robertson

53 ☐ LIGHT OF MY LIFE
Harper

54 ☐ PICTURE PERFECT
Enfield

55 ☐ LOVE ON THE RUN
Graham

56 ☐ ROMANCE IN STORE
Arthur

RIDE THE WINDS OF CHANGE WITH BRENDA COLE'S *ALABAMA MOON* THIS AUGUST.

FIRST LOVE, Department FL/4
1230 Avenue of the Americas
New York, NY 10020

Please send me the books I have checked above. I am enclos-
ing $_____ (please add 50¢ to cover postage and handling.
NYS and NYC residents please add appropriate sales tax).
Send check or money order—no cash or C.O.D.'s please.
Allow six weeks for delivery.

NAME _____

ADDRESS _____

CITY_____ STATE/ZIP_____

First Love from Silhouette

Coming Next Month

Alabama Moon by Brenda Cole

It was bad enough to have her parents divorce. It was worse yet to be shipped out to her aunt's remote farm in Alabama. Why then did it turn out to be the very best summer in Stacy's life?

Some Day My Prince by Veronica Ladd

All her childhood, Maude had told herself fairy stories in which she had starred as the beautiful princess. The prince had been a shadowy, nameless figure. Now that she had finally met Ashley, would he fulfill the role she had dreamed for him?

Double Exposure by Laura Hawkins

How could she have ever stirred up such a hornets' nest? Andrea asked herself. She had annoyed the coach, enraged the principal, alienated her friends and family. Had she also lost forever the one guy she wanted to impress?

A Rainbow For Alison by Maud Johnson

Now that Kirk had appeared, Alison's baby-sitting job had definite possibilities—that is if they could ever be alone together so that she could explore them. Or was he being purposefully dense?